Stewball

The Gabriel Du Pré Series
The Tumbler
Badlands
Ash Child
Cruzatte and Maria
The Stick Game
Long Son
Thunder Horse
Notches
Wolf, No Wolf
Specimen Song
Coyote Wind

The Yellowstone Kelley Series
Kelly and the Three-toed Horse
Imperial Kelly
Kelly Blue
Yellowstone Kelly

Stewball

PETER BOWEN

ST. MARTIN'S MINOTAUR
NEW YORK

www.minotaurbooks.com

Library of Congress Cataloging-in-Publication Data

Bowen, Peter, 1945–
    Stewball : a Gabriel Du Pré mystery / Peter Bowen.
    p. cm.
    ISBN 0-312-27730-X
    EAN 978-0312-27730-7
    1. Du Pré, Gabriel (Fictitious character)—Fiction.   2. Runaway husbands—Fiction.   3. Sheriffs—Fiction.   4. Montana—Fiction. I. Title.

PS3552.O866S74   2005
813'.54—dc22

                    2004056473

First Edition: April 2005

10 9 8 7 6 5 4 3 2 1

For Gatz the Hjortsberg,
a friend who is actually useful

Gabriel Du Pré's Toussaint

GABRIEL DU PRÉ—Metis fiddler, retired brand inspector, solver of puzzles

MADELAINE PLACQUEMINES—Gabriel's woman, children Robert and Thierry (away in Marines) and Lourdes (studying art in Chicago)

JACQUELINE FORTIER—m. Raymond Fortier, twelve children, Du Pré's daughter

MARIA DU PRÉ—Du Pré's daughter, studying overseas

BART FASCELLI—very rich neighbor, alcoholic, runs earthmoving business, money out of Chicago

CHARLES FOOTE—lawyer, troubleshooter for Bart, manages Fascelli empire

BENETSEE—ancient medicine person, mysterious, always been around

BENNY KLEIN—sheriff

SUSAN KLEIN—former schoolteacher, now owns and runs Toussaint Saloon

HARVEY WALLACE—Blackfoot Indian and FBI agent, lives in Washington D.C.

RIPPER—Charles Van Dusen, young agent, mad duck

PALLAS FORTIER—daughter of Jacqueline and Raymond, genius, determined to marry Ripper, if necessary marry his dead body

SAMANTHA PIDGEON—incredibly beautiful and brainy serial killer expert works for FBI, Redbone girl from California

FATHER VAN DEN HEUVEL—Belgian Jesuit, pastor of little Catholic church in Toussaint, physically very inept

JACQUELINE'S CHILDREN—Alcide, Pallas, Lourdes, Marisa & Berne (twins), Hervé, Nepthele, Marie and Barbara (twins), Armand, Gabriel, Colette

PELON—apprentice to Benetsee, often far away on some mysterious business

Stewball

CHAPTER

1

Du Pré and Madelaine and Pallas were standing in the Billings Airport. The lines for the planes were long and the security people were carefully searching everyone and everything.

"You are ten years old," said Madelaine. "Eleven soon. You sure you want to do this?"

Pallas looked at Madelaine.

"Sure," she said. "I am supposed, sit, listen to Mrs. Chalfont tell me seven times six is forty-two? Listen to bad poetry, See Spot fuck Jane?"

"Your mouth," said Madelaine.

Pallas grinned.

"Well," said Madelaine, "all right then."

"I miss you," said Du Pré, looking at Madelaine. She put a hand on his cheek.

Two men in blue blazers led an old woman away, while another carried her bag behind.

"Arabs, they are using seventy-five-year-old women, hijack planes now," said Madelaine. "I am so much safer, these people watching out for me."

"I miss everybody," said Pallas. "But Ripper he is only maybe an hour away."

"I talk Ripper last night," said Madelaine. "Him, he is going to new job."

"Where?" said Pallas. She had decided three years before that Ripper was to be hers and she had been implacably moving after him ever since. Ripper was thirty, an FBI agent, and doomed.

"South Pole," said Madelaine. "He say he hopes to grow old and die there."

"Hah," said Pallas. "Dumb shit think I fall for that."

"You," said Madelaine. "Me, I tell you something. Men, they do not like their women smarter than them. We always are but we don't *say* so."

"Never do," said Du Pré. He and Madelaine looked at each other and laughed.

". . . Flight 497 will be delayed for one hour . . . Flight 497 . . ."

"Ah," said Madelaine, "that little old lady, her girdle is made of dynamite."

Dispirited passengers turned to go to the coffee shop.

"We could maybe drive," said Du Pré.

"Way you drive," said Madelaine, "you be in jail, North Dakota, die of old age there."

"Grandpapa is a very good driver," said Pallas.

"Montana, he is a good driver. Montana, they do not care you drive one-twenty everywhere," said Madelaine. "Other places they get upset, drive like Du Pré."

"There is that Bart," said Du Pré.

"He is ver' rich, always doin' things for people," said Madelaine. "Me, I don't want to use him wrong."

Du Pré nodded.

Bart, him send Madelaine and Pallas, Baltimore, in one of his private jets, him be upset we don't ask.

A cell phone chirred and Pallas took it out of her backpack. She listened.

"Yes," she said. "Yes. They are being, you know, polite."

She listened some more.

"It is true, both assholes," said Pallas. "You want, tell them that?"

Du Pré and Madelaine looked down at Pallas, who looked up and grinned.

"Uncle Bart thinks you are assholes," she said. She handed the phone to Du Pré.

"You hurt my feelings," said Bart.

"Madelaine, she does not want, treat you bad," said Du Pré.

"I understand," said Bart. "Now give me Madelaine."

Du Pré handed the telephone to Madelaine.

"Bart," she said, "you are too good, don't want—"

She listened, a smile tugging at the corner of her mouth.

"I don't mean that, you know," she said.

She listened some more.

"OK, OK," said Madelaine. "You don't shit your pants on me now."

Du Pré looked at the ceiling, grinning.

Madelaine handed the phone to Du Pré.

"Don't do this again," said Bart. "It isn't safe, they aren't safe, you know what a bunch of bozos we got these days."

"OK," said Du Pré. "So what?"

"Foote was in Seattle seeing to something," said Bart, "so he will touch down at Billings in forty-five minutes, the plane will drop him off in Chicago, and then take Madelaine and Pallas on—"

"OK," said Du Pré.

"I appreciate your trying to be polite," said Bart. "I do not appreciate my friends sneaking around on me."

"I am sorry," said Du Pré.

"I know it is Madelaine," said Bart, "and I love her for it, but please don't do this again."

"You talk, her," said Du Pré.

He handed the cell phone to Madelaine.

She listened for a moment.

"OK," she said. "You are right I was being selfish, thinking I am a good person."

"Thank you," said Bart. "Now may I speak to the monster?"

Madelaine handed the telephone to Pallas.

"Uncle Bart," said Pallas.

"Now," said Bart, "you will not fail to call me if you need anything?"

"I promise," said Pallas. "I call you from the john here, don't I?"

Du Pré looked down at his granddaughter.

"Little shit," said Madelaine.

"They are getting old and slow," said Pallas. "Neither one of them figure it out till now, Uncle Bart. You take good care of them, they maybe start drooling and not remembering so good soon. Me, I hate to go off, leave them to themselves, it is probably dangerous, them."

"It is very good of you to be so concerned about your grandparents," said Bart. "And I am sure that they appreciate it—"

"Hang up," said Madelaine. "Me, I got a neck to break."

"She is going, break my neck," said Pallas.

"You can hardly blame her," said Bart, "all things considered."

"Bye," said Pallas. "Madelaine, she is gettin' red, bad sign."

"Make tracks," said Bart.

Pallas lunged for safety. Madelaine was a little faster and got a grip on the scruff of her neck.

People in the airport looked on, dismayed.

Madelaine lifted Pallas one-handed so they saw eye to eye.

"Ver' funny," she said. "Me, I am laughing."

"You better put me down," said Pallas. "You don't there will be a dozen social workers coming through that door, help—"

Madelaine set Pallas down. The two women beamed at each other.

"You are not a little girl," said Madelaine.

"Yeah," said Pallas. "Well, it is good disguise, last a little while."
She took Madelaine's hand and she laughed happily.

The busybodies looked away.

"I really miss you, I am there, Baltimore," said Pallas.

"Sure," said Madelaine. "Me, though, I not have so much headaches."

"I am not that bad," said Pallas.

"Yes," said Madelaine, "you are. Now you are not to play tricks, Ripper. He is dead meat already, it is not fair."

"I don't want him forget me," said Pallas.

"He is not going to forget you," said Madelaine. "Him, he tell me he wakes up in the night sweating and screaming, always dreaming of you."

"He is so sweet," said Pallas.

"Him be there, you land, Baltimore," said Madelaine.

"That is ver' nice, him," said Pallas.

"Nice," said Madelaine, "his butt. Him just want to give you a present."

"Sweet," said Pallas.

"It is an ankle bracelet," said Madelaine. "Tells him where you are all of the time."

"Oh," said Pallas.

"What you want?" said Madelaine. "Platinum, little plates, say, I love you truly?"

"You are kidding," said Pallas.

"I may be," said Madelaine. "But Ripper, he is not."

"Won't do him any good," said Pallas.

"I am going to the car," said Du Pré. "There is something there I forgot."

Du Pré found his old cruiser in the lot. He fished the bottle from under the seat, and he had some bourbon. Then he had some more.

He looked at the airport building, and he began to laugh.

CHAPTER

2

Du Pré pulled into Toussaint and to the saloon, and he parked where he usually did by the side door. It was a pleasant day, cool for August, and he walked to the front of the saloon and he looked at all of the flowers in the boxes that the owner, Susan Klein, kept there. She was able to get prairie flowers to grow in the boxes, which very few people could do.

Du Pré glanced at the cars. One plate was Canadian, Alberta, and the car was dusty, and had been driven a long way recently. One headlight had been knocked out.

There was a hat on the back ledge, dark red, with a silver-and-gold band and a peacock feather at the clasp.

Du Pré frowned.

He sighed and he went into the saloon.

His Auntie Pauline was sitting on a stool. Her fringed jacket swayed a little as she turned to look.

Du Pré slid up on a stool beside her.

Trouble woman now she got trouble will soon be mine . . . shit . . .

Susan Klein set a ditchwater highball in front of Du Pré and a bowl of salted peanuts.

"Eat?" she said.

Du Pré nodded.

"They off all right?" said Susan.

Du Pré nodded and Susan went to the kitchen to make Du Pré a cheeseburger.

Auntie Pauline looked at Du Pré with her black eyes. Her makeup was very heavy. She was sixty and she did not like it.

"OK," said Du Pré. "You drive down, all this way, what trouble you got?"

"My husband," she said. "He disappeared. Him down here someplace."

Du Pré looked at her.

"You got a husband run off," said Du Pré. "Husbands they do that. Him is what? Fifth? More?"

"I don't drive down here listen to you be a pig," said Auntie Pauline. "Him get in some trouble, he have to go maybe find out some things, tell your FBI about them, but he is gone now two weeks and he was to be back four days ago and he is not, so maybe he is now in some trouble."

Du Pré took a long pull on his drink.

. . . trouble woman, my father kill Bart's brother over her, she has one man she says, you go now, blow his brains out, and she is sixty and last two husbands I meet are maybe thirty . . . trouble woman, my aunt . . .

"Him working for the FBI, eh?" said Du Pré. "Now, they tell you that, or him, he tell you that?"

"Pig," said Auntie Pauline.

"Yes," said Du Pré. "You got these husbands, change like you do underwear, and me, I think maybe he just get scared and run, yes?"

"Bullshit," said Pauline. "This is not a lie."

"So," said Du Pré, "this husband is someplace, America, me, I find him for you you think."

"You know people," said Auntie Pauline. "I talk to Madelaine, she tell me come."

. . . Madelaine believe her, well. . . .

"OK," said Du Pré. "You stay here maybe, couple days, I see what I can do."

Susan Klein brought the cheeseburger, and Du Pré ate.

"Madelaine tell me stay at her place," said Auntie Pauline.

Du Pré nodded. Madelaine would say that. She don't say dick to me, but she say that.

"She said I call you, you hang up," said Auntie Pauline.

Du Pré nodded and had another bite of cheeseburger.

"But Badger, he will not just go off and not tell me, he told me he had to come down here, do something, or he is going to jail, so . . ." said Auntie Pauline.

Du Pré wolfed down the french fries. Susan Klein brought him another drink.

"Badger, he loves me," said Pauline. "Now, I don't need crap, you, I need help, Badger he is in trouble maybe, and me, I want you, find him."

Pauline stood up and she put five dollars on the bartop.

Canadian five.

She went out the door.

Susan picked up the bill.

"She," said Susan, "is one fell creature." Susan had been the schoolteacher for many years, until she bought the bar because it was less trouble.

Du Pré snorted.

Fierce tiger fell . . . me, I remember that poem, trying to help my Maria understand it when I don't . . . *fell* . . .

"Deadly," said Susan Klein. "Beautiful and deadly."

Du Pré laughed.

"She is that," he said.

"Who is she exactly?" said Susan. "If I am not being too nosey . . ."

Du Pré shook his head.

"My aunt," said Du Pré, "two years younger than me. My grand-papa he marry after his wife dies, young woman, then my grandfather dies, she is still young, she has Pauline, catch colt . . ."

"Ah," said Susan.

"She is very beautiful, rodeo queen, makes four, five movies," said Du Pré. "Not big parts, but she has them, gets married, divorced, married, divorced, is in that Hollywood a while, comes back, Canada, goes on being married, divorced . . ."

Susan Klein looked at Du Pré.

"She is the one Catfoot killed Gianni Fascelli over," she said.

"Yes," said Du Pré. "Long time gone."

"Too beautiful," said Susan. "Too beautiful for herself anyway."

Du Pré nodded.

"It won't be the same without Pallas about," said Susan. "She is one little pistol. I had bright kids in my classes but she is somethin' else."

"Yes," said Du Pré.

"She is going to be a really beautiful woman, too," said Susan. "Is she still deadly determined to have poor Ripper?"

Du Pré nodded.

"He could shoot himself I suppose," said Susan.

"Him, he think she come to her senses," said Du Pré. "She decides it is him she is seven, that is that."

"Pallas has a good heart," said Susan. "You know, Ripper is really a lucky guy. She's a real genius and she has so much love in her."

"Guy gets told by some kid he is it, luck is not what he thinks first off," said Du Pré.

Susan laughed.

Her husband, Benny, the county sheriff, came in. He was whistling.

He slid up on a stool by Du Pré, stood on the rungs, and leaned over to kiss Susan.

"How's lawn forcement?" said Susan.

"Quiet," said Benny. "Very quiet, which is the best."

Benny hated to arrest people, and he was made sick by death. So he was the best man for the job.

"Du Pré's pistol of an aunt is down here," said Susan, "which is why he looks like his dog died."

"Pauline?" said Benny.

Du Pré nodded.

Benny laughed.

"I like her," he said. "I think she's good folks."

Du Pré nodded.

"She is worried about her husband," said Susan.

"Oh," said Benny, his soft heart crossing his forehead.

"I will be out, Bart's," said Du Pré. "Pauline, she will be at Madelaine's."

He went out and got into his cruiser.

"Shit. Damn," he said as he drove away.

CHAPTER

3

The telephone rang and Du Pré nodded at Booger Tom, the old cowpoke, and he went to the phone on the wall of the kitchen.

"Yes," said Du Pré.

"You called me," said Harvey Wallace, Blackfeet and FBI.

"Yah," said Du Pré.

"Unusual," said Harvey. "Usually I call you. Usually you take to the weeds and do not wish to talk to me."

"Usually," said Du Pré, "you call I am up to my ears in shit next day, get shot at, am doing things I am too old for, never liked in the first place."

"I owe you one," said Harvey.

"You owe me about twenty," said Du Pré.

"We could haggle," said Harvey.

"My Auntie Pauline she is down, Canada, tells me her husband who is called Badger is working, you, and Badger he is missing," said Du Pré.

Harvey was silent for a very long time.

"The excellent Badger," said Harvey.

So he knew what Du Pré was talking about.

"So," said Du Pré, "I think she is giving me bullshit this Badger is working, you. Auntie Pauline, she eats men and tosses the husks out the window after she wipes her ass with them, and me, I think this is bullshit, Badger just take off, maybe not get used to wipe her ass, but you say maybe he did not. Him working, you?"

"I can't talk about this," said Harvey.

"Fine," said Du Pré. "So what is this anyway?"

Someone came into Harvey's office and Harvey put a hand over the telephone and he was gone for three minutes.

"Sorry," he said. "Now, I really didn't know Badger was related to you."

"Why would you?" said Du Pré. "So he is dead, you tell me."

"Yeah," said Harvey. "We found him last night."

"OK," said Du Pré. "Where?"

"Down in Wyoming," said Harvey.

"You need this Badger," said Du Pré. "So you convince him work for you, so what is it that he does, you convince him with."

"Drugs," said Harvey. "He came across the border with a load of Canadian blue Valium, enough for a whole lot of felonies, and so—"

"So you twist his nuts, and get you some dope dealers," said Du Pré.

"No," said Harvey. "The Canadians rolled up the other end and we got this one, and poor old Badger was flying lone when we got him. Of course, both ends were more than happy to tell us where poor old Badger was and what he had, in hopes of a light sentence. Badger, well, he had hopes, too."

"Who is this Badger?" said Du Pré.

"Really not a bad guy," said Harvey. "He was a diesel mechanic and damn good at it, had a bad divorce five years ago, cost him a lot, so he was ripe to do a little driving. You know how that is."

"Yah," said Du Pré.

"So," said Harvey, "I have been after this bunch for a while, and I thought maybe I could give old Badger a legend and a couple mil and he could give me them."

"Jesus," said Du Pré.

"Badger was a good guy, just screwed up a couple times," said Harvey. "I knew if he said he'd do it, he'd try, you see."

"OK," said Du Pré.

"And that is all I will say right now," said Harvey. "But if you were to, say, drive down to the Wind River country, stay at the Motel Six in Riverton, I will be there first thing in the morning."

"Shit," said Du Pré.

"Look," said Harvey. "This is outside the fence, you know."

"Yeah," said Du Pré.

Harvey had a way of handing things over the fence to Du Pré that no one on his side of the fence could do anything with.

"Look," said Harvey, "is that miserable old goat Booger Tom still living?"

Du Pré looked at Booger Tom.

"I think so," said Du Pré. "He is breathing anyway."

The old cowboy raised his head and put a cold blue eye on Du Pré.

"Who you talkin' to?" said Booger Tom. "That I should know about?"

"Harvey Wallace," said Du Pré.

"Oh," said Booger Tom. "Ask him how things is in the secret police." Booger Tom regarded the Federal Government as a loathsome and wholly unnecessary welfare scam.

"See if he would come down to Riverton with you," said Harvey.

"You see," said Du Pré, handing the telephone to Booger Tom.

Harvey said some things.

Booger Tom listened.

"All I want out of this," he said, "is that flap-eared dwarf we got in the White House kiss my ass at high noon on the steps of the Capitol."

Harvey said some more things.

"We ain't had one worth a shit since Teddy Roosevelt," said Booger Tom.

Harvey Wallace said some more things.

"You all so busy trying to catch A-rabs you don't got time for this or what?" said Booger Tom.

Harvey Wallace said some more things.

"Now," said Booger Tom, "durned if I don't find that interesting."

Harvey said some more things.

"Oh," said Booger Tom. "You know about that."

Harvey said some more things.

"I pawned the goddamned thing," said Booger Tom.

Harvey said some more things.

"If memory serves," said Booger Tom. "About seven bucks."

He handed the telephone back to Du Pré.

Harvey was still laughing.

"Huh?" said Du Pré.

"You know that old bastard got the Congressional Medal of Honor for valor at Heartbreak Ridge? Korea," said Harvey.

"It was not," said Du Pré. "It was the Spanish-American War."

Harvey said a few more things.

"Oh," said Du Pré.

". . . so tomorrow morning," said Harvey. "In Riverton."

Du Pré hung up.

"Here 'n' you thought that Madelaine was goin' off for a month with that brat and life would be quiet," said Booger Tom.

"No," said Du Pré.

"Interestin' he would want to know what he wants to know," said Booger Tom. "I suppose we can talk it out on the way."

"You are goin'?" said Du Pré.

Booger Tom nodded.

"I kin act rich I have to," he said.

The old man was excited.

Du Pré shook his head.

"I don't know I want to do this," he said.

Booger Tom snorted.

They grinned at each other.

They packed their things in Du Pré's old cruiser. Booger Tom brought out a case of Canadian whiskey.

Bart came back, driving the huge truck with his dragline on it. He was worth a lot of money, and he liked digging holes in the ground.

"They got there fine," said Bart. "Madelaine said it was an easy trip."

Du Pré nodded.

"Where are you two off to?" said Bart.

"None a yer business, ya fat guinea prick," said Booger Tom.

"OK," said Bart. "Call, you find work."

CHAPTER

4

Du Pré pulled into the parking lot of the motel at dawn. Booger Tom had slept for a few hours, and the old man was breathing gently. He did not stir when Du Pré shut off the engine.

Harvey and two other men stood by a green SUV.

Du Pré yawned and he got out and stood and stretched, and then he walked over to the FBI agents.

"Mornin'," said Harvey.

He introduced the two younger men and Du Pré forgot their names immediately.

Then the two younger agents got into the green SUV and they drove off.

Harvey had a stout canvas suitcase with leather bracing and trim and he picked it up and they walked to Du Pré's old cruiser. Harvey got in back. He slid the suitcase over on top of Booger Tom's and Du Pré's stuff.

The old cowboy stirred and yawned.

He looked out the window.

"Riverton, Wyoming," he said. "I was in the jail here once. Just a two-star hoosegow."

"Two stars," said Harvey.

"Baloney three times a day," said Booger Tom, "and the coffee was terrible."

Du Pré and Harvey laughed.

Harvey pointed south and Du Pré headed out of town. He stopped at a gas station and he filled up the tank and he put a quart of oil in the engine and he topped off the radiator coolant.

Harvey came back from the little convenience store with three cups of coffee.

He pointed south again and Du Pré drove.

The green SUV was waiting fifteen miles south of town, on a dirt road that went east.

They drove for half an hour, up and over a low range of hills. There was a wide basin beyond, and cattle were browsing in the salt-sage flats.

They followed the green SUV over a double path worn down into the land.

There was a flat place at the bottom, and they parked there and got out.

There were many tire tracks, of trucks and trailers.

"So," said Harvey, taking a manila envelope out of a side pocket on his suitcase, "Badger was there, about a hundred yards off . . ."

He pulled out some photographs and he handed them to Du Pré.

The younger agents looked at each other, and one shrugged.

"You don't like it," said Harvey amiably, "why don't you go call the ratline and file a complaint?"

The two younger men flushed.

Du Pré looked at the photographs. Badger had been found lying on his back with his arms flung out and his feet crossed.

"Shot once, base of the skull," said Harvey.

Executed.

"OK," said Du Pré. "So what is this we are looking at here?"

"There were a bunch of people here," said Harvey, "all about the same time, two mornings ago. We don't know who they were or why they were here. It isn't what you would expect. There were . . . how many vehicles?" Harvey looked at the younger agents.

"We counted forty-eight," one said. "From the tires."

"Special film," said Harvey. "Gives great contrast on disturbed earth."

"So," said Du Pré. "So what is it that you want?"

"Harvey," said Booger Tom, "you ain't tellin' us why Badger was here or much of anything. It is easy to see what went on here you got eyes."

Harvey looked at the old cowboy.

"But I ain't tellin' you dick, you don't let me in on what you got," said Booger Tom.

Harvey nodded.

"You can go," he said to the younger agents. "Have a good time on the ratline."

"Christ, Harvey," said one of the agents. "It is just this is against all the regs, and we aren't big guys like you."

"We're little kahunas," said the other, "and this could bend our files wrong, you know."

Harvey jingled the change in his pockets.

"Since nine-eleven," he said, "there has been an increasing hunger our bosses feel for results."

The younger men looked at each other.

"Right," one said.

"And fewer of us doing other than looking for terrorists," said Harvey. "I think we are well beneath the radar."

The younger men both nodded.

"So," said Harvey, "I am going to tell these two, and then they are going to tell us what it was that went on here."

The younger agents looked at each other and threw up their hands.

"Badger was carrying a lot of money," said Harvey, "because we

18

had a very strange thing happen. Seems that down in New Mexico this old bastard of a rancher put a quarter mil into his bank account, and all hundreds, which of course meant that Treasury was notified. That much in hundreds, well, it is dope, sure as shit, but even better, the hundreds were rumored to be counterfeit."

Du Pré and Booger Tom looked at Harvey.

"Now, his banker is said to have asked questions of the rancher, who simply said he had no idea why they were bad bills, hadn't meant to do anything to anyone, and he would like them back so he could burn them. Banker—who was a life-long friend—gave them to him before Treasury got wind of their nature, and sure as shit the rancher torched the lot. Time the Treasury boys caught up, the evidence was ashes and the rancher, oddly enough, didn't seem to give much of a shit that somebody had paid him off with bogus hundreds—not that he was admitting they *were*. Banker stayed mum and Treasury was baffled. Matter of fact they were so baffled they actually told us about it in the fond hope we had something to do with it, but we did not. So there we were with this rumor of a crime but no evidence except the bank's testimony and deposit and withdrawal records, but the bills were long gone and the guy got stung just didn't care that he'd been handed a quarter mil in bad paper. Now, this was curious, very curious, and we turned the guy's life upside down, but all we found was a decent tax-paying citizen had a big ranch and some bucks. So we thought it was gambling, since that was all that made sense. The guy didn't need to deal dope, which is as you know risky, and so that made no sense, and he had a good lawyer who advised him to keep his yap shut, which he did, other than to say what does it matter if I don't give a shit?"

Du Pré and Booger Tom nodded.

"So we send Badger off with two mil in marked hundreds," said Harvey, "and make him a dot-com millionaire, and he takes off on his own, and maybe he finds something and maybe not, and he is gone eight whole days. Then a rancher flying over sees the coyotes eating him down here, and in time it is known that Badger is one of ours and so we are called. Nice of them. Treasury by now don't know us or anything about this and so . . . Here I am with a dead informant who was doing something I know not what, and it bothers me. Like I said, I didn't think Badger was a bad sort. He was smart and he said he'd get us something we never even thought of if we would sort of forget the thirty thousand tabs of Canadian Blue he had with him when he was ratted out."

Harvey took out a box of small, very smelly cigars, and he lit one and smoked.

Booger Tom was walking into the sagebrush now, and he got about a hundred feet away and he knelt down for a time. Then he came back.

"I even thought of stolen horses," said Harvey, "but there isn't enough money in horses for this . . . unless you are talking thoroughbreds."

Booger Tom looked at Harvey and he laughed.

"You know what this is, Du Pré?" said Booger Tom.

"Maybe," said Du Pré. "But you are full of it, so maybe you tell us."

"Had a brush race here," said Booger Tom. "A brush race, and somewheres in it somebody took a dislike of your feller Badger."

"A brush race," said Harvey.

"Yup," said Booger Tom. "And let me guess, when you sent pore ol' Badger off with the two mil, I expect them bills was counterfeit."

The two younger agents turned beet red.

"Yup," said Harvey, glaring at them. "You assholes want to go call the ratline *now?*"

CHAPTER

5

"Bureaucratic man," said Harvey. "That is a creature which has managed to remove from its self its spine, decency, honor, and brain. It exists to exist. Now, I would bet you would like some of the rest of the story. One of those two young pups we had with us out there is Randall Warner. His father saved my life once, and then, a few years ago, Jack Warner jumped in front of a woman when a bust went bad and he took the bullet. Killed him. Didn't kill him for a while, though, and he asked me to look after Randall. I have tried."

Du Pré and Harvey and Booger Tom were in a roadhouse south of Riverton sipping drinks. The steaks had been good and the potatoes had been good and the vegetables had been simmering so long they were transparent and flat, but then vegetables, as Booger Tom said, was what you *fed* to food.

Du Pré nodded.

"So Randall was on this, and a fine bureaucrat gave him the money, without telling him that it was bogus, and so Randall handed it off like a good boy to Badger, and I hope out of all of this he learns never to trust no one no how no time at all . . ."

"That," said Booger Tom, "is about disgusting."

Harvey nodded.

"The FBI has such a long and honorable history," said Harvey. "You ever hear about the Kanasas City Massacre? That was great. Some thugs were being taken to the federal pen at Leavenworth, back in 1933, and some other thugs tried, it was said, to bust them out. Big shootout in the street by the train station. Several dead, cops and prisoners, but then, when they added up the evidence, it pointed to an FBI agent named Lackey who had grabbed the wrong gun, one that he didn't know, and so the good agent Lackey blew away the prisoner and two cops by accident. The rising young head of the FBI was that swell fellow Jedgar Hoover and legend has it he blamed it all on Pretty Boy Floyd, who was three hundred miles away, and then had Floyd gunned down so he wouldn't spoil anything by way of telling the truth. Ol' Jedgar used this mess to get a law passed so his agents could carry guns. You want to see bureaucratic man at his most evolved, Jedgar is hard to beat."

"Why you stay there?" said Du Pré.

Harvey looked at his glass.

"If we wait for perfection in man," he said, "we will wait a very long time and much will be lost that need not be. Thomas Jefferson—"

"What you gonna do about the prick gave Randall the counterfeit bills?" said Booger Tom.

"After we get to the bottom of this, or, rather, you do," said Harvey, "I will contact our fine free press, very quietly, and point them in the right direction."

Du Pré nodded.

. . . no fucking wonder we are in this. Harvey sends his people, the guy handed off the bad bills will smell it and fuck it up . . .

"So," said Harvey, "I actually need this as a favor."

"Sure," said Booger Tom. "Happy to 'blige."

Harvey nodded, and he stood up.

"More than this," he said, "I will not know."

Du Pré looked up.

"We get runnin' money from Bart," said Booger Tom.

Harvey nodded.

"What else?" said Du Pré.

"You may find out some things that will make you very mad at our fine government," said Harvey.

"Couldn't make me *any* madder," said Booger Tom.

Du Pré got up and he walked out with Harvey, who stood by a tan government sedan.

"You know Badger was married to my aunt?" said Du Pré.

"I did not know shit about this," said Harvey, "till Randall called me. He was plenty angry, and he had the smarts to be plenty scared. There have been so many glorious fuckups in our fine Federal Bureau of Investigation of late that the ass-coverers are knifing anyone they can get a shiv into, and the stupid prick that set this one up knows he's got a bad problem. So there we are."

"So you are asking this for friendship," said Du Pré.

Harvey nodded.

"OK," said Du Pré. "Now I will do it."

Harvey nodded.

"You'd have liked Warner," said Harvey. "God knows I did."

"This guy," said Du Pré, "him maybe sending somebody on his own?"

"Nah," said Harvey. "He wants it buried. Deep. No, he will be sniffing around, but he won't risk sending any of our folk, and he would not know anyone else, on account of he is such a repulsive asshole, unlike me."

"OK," said Du Pré.

"My wife said Madelaine and Pallas are coming to supper," said Harvey. "So she's a math genius, eh?"

"Yeah," said Du Pré.

"Poor Ripper," said Harvey. "I keep telling him suicide is his only hope and he gets rude—"

"He has time," said Du Pré. "Five years she will be sixteen . . ."

"Uh-huh," said Harvey.

"How bad is it?" said Du Pré, looking hard at him.

"Bad. Gets worse, gets better," said Harvey.

They shook hands.

"I know this leads someplace," said Harvey, "but I can't send my dogs."

"Yah," said Du Pré. "I see that."

Harvey got into the sedan and he started the engine and pulled out and he was soon gone in the dark, headed toward Denver.

Booger Tom came out of the roadhouse.

"I have this feeling," said Booger Tom, "that he ain't telling us all of what he knows."

Du Pré shook his head.

"He has some rat in the pantry," said Du Pré.

"OK," said Booger Tom. "If you buy it, I do. Now, thing is we got to get us some runnin' money, and I got to go home and make some calls on some fellers I used to know."

Du Pré nodded.

Booger Tom handed Du Pré a manila envelope.

Du Pré got in his cruiser and pulled the papers out, and he looked at them under the dome light.

The bullet that had killed Badger had been ceramic and was untraceable, for it had broken into dust.

"See-ramic bullet," said Booger Tom.

The sort used for indoor target practice, or to shoot rats in the basement, since they would not ricochet.

"I have never seen one," said Du Pré.

"I got a couple boxes," said Booger Tom. "Use 'em under the house and the barn where the stonework is. They work fine but you got to hit what you are aiming at."

Du Pré shoved the report back in the envelope.

"So," he said. "We drive home."

The old man made a pillow of his jacket and he went to sleep and Du Pré headed north. As soon as the road was a silver ribbon across emptiness, he cranked it up.

They got back to Toussaint in midmorning.

Du Pré yawned. He hadn't slept a lot in two days.

Du Pré drove up on the bench south of the Wolf Mountains where Bart's ranch was, and he and Booger Tom went to the house and ate some lunch and then they slept.

They slept a long time, and when Du Pré awoke it was early the next morning.

CHAPTER

6

Du Pré sighed as he got out of his cruiser. He went to the white gate in the picket fence and up the walk to Madelaine's front door and he knocked and ten minutes later Auntie Pauline opened the door, her makeup on though she was dressed in a robe.

"He is dead," she said flatly.

"Yes," said Du Pré.

Auntie Pauline turned without a word and she went to the kitchen and she poured some whiskey into a glass and she drank it down neat without stopping to swallow or breathe.

"He was a nice man," said Pauline.

Du Pré poured himself some whiskey.

"I knew it. I know it a while," said Pauline. "That damn Badger him, he is hauling dope, the stupid shit. He is not smart enough to do it. I tell him that, he laugh and say, how smart you got to be, drive over the border? They don't check much, America, Canada."

Du Pré nodded.

Even with the supposed added security anyone could go across the border with Canada about anywhere any time without anyone caring very much. Catfoot had hauled bootleg over the border, even hauled moonshine back to Canada when the price was right.

"So how it happens?" said Pauline.

"Somebody shoot him, Wyoming," said Du Pré.

Pauline nodded.

"He calls me they are letting him out. He says he will be back soon as he does this thing that he has to do, them, and then he will be home. I say what it is you have to do? He won't tell me."

Du Pré nodded.

"He calls you from the jail?" said Du Pré.

Pauline shook her head.

"Calls from jail it is collect," she said. "Him, he calling from someplace else because he just call me, you know."

Du Pré sucked down another large draft of whiskey.

"He is doing something, them FBI," said Pauline. "They cut a deal he does this thing for them and then they don't keep him in jail long time."

"When did he get arrested?" said Du Pré.

"Spring," said Pauline. "March, I think now, yes, and he is in the jail a while while they are thinking of something for him to do."

Du Pré nodded.

"He call you from the jail collect," said Du Pré, "so where is this he is calling from?"

"Minneapolis," said Pauline. "Sometimes Denver."

Du Pré looked at her.

"You got those telephone bills?" he said.

She nodded.

"You get home," said Du Pré, "you send them to me, they are important."

"OK," said Pauline. "I think I got them, my desk."

"Very important maybe," said Du Pré.

Pauline nodded.

"What they do, his body?" she said.

"Evidence," said Du Pré. "They keep it a while, maybe a trial."

Pauline nodded.

"I go home then," she said. She went off and she was soon back in her leather outfit, the fringed jacket and the leather pants and the high-tooled boots and the silver and gold jewelry.

"Old rodeo queen," said Pauline. "Maybe I don't get married again."

Pauline had her suitcase packed and her vanity case with her war paints.

Du Pré carried them out.

Auntie Pauline had never been very domestic and the sink was full of dirty dishes, but she was always like that.

She started the car.

"You got money, get home?" said Du Pré.

"Maybe," said Pauline. "I don't I peddle pussy, the truckers." She looked up at Du Pré and she was smiling.

She liked to shock, too. She always had.

Du Pré fished a hundred dollars out of his wallet and he gave it to her.

She tucked it in her shirt pocket. Then she patted Du Pré's hand.

"I am an old whore," she said. "But it is not so bad, you know, I have had some ver' good times."

Too beautiful for her heart.

"You do all right," said Du Pré.

Pauline drove off then, and she waved once with her left hand, out the window, graceful, a single motion.

Du Pré shook his head, laughing.

Auntie Pauline stories.

She makes good stories.

Du Pré went into Madelaine's house and he fished the scrapbook down from the closet shelf and he took it to the kitchen and he set it on the table and he poured himself some more whiskey.

There were his baby pictures, which Madelaine had told him

had to stay, and then some pictures of Catfoot and Mama, young, very handsome they were, and others aging, and then three pages of Auntie Pauline, who was stunningly beautiful as a young woman.

She was laughing in most of them, white teeth, full lips, very dark hair, high cheekbones. She had been a good horsewoman; she rode around the arena while the crowd roared and the men stared at her ass.

There were a few head shots from Pauline's starlet days, but not very many.

"She was hooking," said Du Pré aloud.

He laughed.

Better than Auntie Suzanne, who became a nun and who spent her life beating little palms with a ruler in a school in Manitoba.

But men had been a trouble to Auntie Pauline, men in Hollywood and then Gianni Fascelli and then the younger ones she had married.

Trouble woman, most of the trouble was her own.

Du Pré sighed.

He looked at the young pictures of Pauline, the days when she turned men's heads in the street and Du Pré remembered she had caused a car wreck once, just walking in front of a man who was so smitten he drove into a power pole.

She had been a very beautiful young woman, but it was a burden to her. Her life had been broken up into each man's time, and she had nothing left now.

"She will marry again," Du Pré said.

She would, too.

Du Pré sighed. He closed the album before he got to his wedding pictures, his wife dead of leukemia when the girls were so small.

. . . I was someone else then, I am not him now, I love Madelaine . . .

He put the album back up on the shelf and he went out to his cruiser and he drove out to Bart's.

Bart and Booger Tom were on the front deck, and they both waved when Du Pré drove in.

He got out and he went up the steps.

"This old bastard wants two million bucks," said Bart, "and even more to buy horses with."

"I kin make more money with this than you kin with this beef," said Booger Tom.

"I don't need to make money," said Bart.

"OK," said Booger Tom. "I kin lose a bunch, I promise."

"Illegal horse races," said Bart, "do not make for tax breaks."

"You don't give a shit about money," said Booger Tom.

"No," said Bart. "Now what is this all about, really?"

Du Pré got some coffee and he sat down.

"Harvey," he began . . .

CHAPTER

7

"Harvey's after somebody in the FBI," said Foote, Bart's ferocious lawyer, all the more so because of his mild appearance. Du Pré had reached him by phone in his Washington office.

"Yah," said Du Pré. "But this business with the counterfeit money bothers me. Guy puts a quarter of a million, bad bills, a bank, and takes it out and burns it and that is that. Counterfeit money, it is illegal."

"But a case could be made," said Foote, "that there was no felonious attempt to pass it off as real, no complaint by the fellow, and after he torched it, no evidence. Yes, it stinks, but it would be hard to get an indictment by saying so."

"Me," said Du Pré, "I do not like doing things I don't know what it is I am doing, don't know all of it."

"Nor do I," said Foote, "but Harvey approached us and so did a government official whom I trust. What Harvey asked you to do was find the illegal horse races and bet heavily and see what happens."

"And buy horses to race," said Du Pré.

"Which I am sure you can do," said Foote.

"Not so simple," said Du Pré. "Brush races, they are for quarter horses. There are lots of quarter horses, but not that many good racing ones, like any race deal, and they are known. We maybe find a colt and train him, but that takes at least two years, maybe three. So, we don't have that time, we got to find two, three good horses, already trained, and there are not that many."

"I understand," said Foote. "But we have your horses."

"What?" said Du Pré.

"Harvey did not give you your new identities yet?" said Foote. "Booger Tom is Dave Wilson, an American who went to Australia right after World War Two. You are his assistant, one Armand Dumont, whom he hired. Wilson made his fortune in mining and now he is returning to America to race."

"There are lots of quarter horses in Australia," said Du Pré.

"I would not know," said Foote. "Harvey asked for help. Seems he does not trust his own Bureau."

"What else is there in this I am not being told?" said Du Pré.

"Well," said Foote, "I haven't been told it, either, but let us speculate. This much effort would not be expended upon an informant of . . . Badger's . . . ah . . . caliber. Which is not to say poor Badger was after something unimportant, only that *he* was unimportant. Badger was the best they had at the moment. There is, I gather, a great deal of money bet upon these races. Now, let us suppose that someone wished to cover the tracks of some money brought into this country. Small amounts may be run through casinos, where one purchases a few tens of thousands of dollars worth of chips, gambles hardly at all, and cashes them in the next day or so for bills which are commingled and untraceable. But that has its limits. But if one were to bring in millions of dollars, and contrive to lose them to an accomplice . . ."

"OK," said Du Pré.

"Gabriel," said Foote, "I know you fairly well. No doubt I have told you nothing you did not already think of. I don't know much about this, but the fellow who asked for our help I do know and trust, so it is upon that we agreed to do this. It is dangerous, as poor Badger has demonstrated."

"Yah," said Du Pré. "But him, him pass the bad money and he does not know that it is, and somebody gets really mad and kills him, so maybe this does not have anything to do with anything more than that."

"Possible," said Foote.

"So this money, it is coming from drugs?" said Du Pré.

"I don't know," said Foote.

"You do not," said Du Pré.

"I think that is what we wish to find out," said Foote.

"I should do this thing?" said Du Pré.

"Yes," said Foote.

"It is important, not just this money?" said Du Pré.

Foote sighed.

"I would think it is very important," he said. "I had a sense of great urgency, but in these matters nothing is admitted to which does not have to be admitted to."

"Bart knows about this," said Du Pré.

"Of course," said Foote. "It is, after all, his money."

"So we find these races," said Du Pré, "which is maybe pretty easy to do. We race horses, we bet, maybe we lose, maybe win. What do we do then?"

"I would think," said Foote, "that Harvey's people would be right behind you."

"OK," said Du Pré.

"I do not know much," said Foote, "but the man who asked for our help would not ask if it were not very, very important."

"OK," said Du Pré. He hung up the telephone.

Booger Tom was out by the round corral, leaning against the rail fence, smoking a handrolled cigarette.

Du Pré went out to the corral and he rolled a cigarette and lit it.

"Some shit, ain't it?" said Booger Tom. "Well, I suppose we ought to."

"Yah," said Du Pré.

"Whatever this is," said Booger Tom, "it ain't about how fast a horse can run and which horse can run fastest, now is it?"

Du Pré shook his head.

"So you get that Medal of Honor?" said Du Pré.

"Sure did," said Booger Tom. "They said I was this here hero, but I only done what I did 'cause there was this Commie tank in the only place I had to run *to*."

Du Pré nodded.

"Got seven bucks for it," said Booger Tom. "Or was it eleven?"

Du Pré nodded.

"All bullshit anyway," said Booger Tom.

Du Pré nodded.

"So," said Booger Tom. "Time to go and get the mail."

He walked down the half mile of road toward the big metal mailbox, set up on some welded chain snaking out over the road so the snowplows would not knock it over.

The telephone rang, and Du Pré went into the house and picked it up.

"Yah?" he said.

"It is Madelaine," said Madelaine. "This is a ver' strange place. Houses, they are about twelve feet apart. Streets, they look like sheep pounds for dipping. The air is brown, and I don't like it so much."

"You are there a month," said Du Pré. "Jacqueline will not let Pallas stay there you don't stay."

"She say that," said Madelaine, "I talk to her."

"She *mean* that," said Du Pré. "I know my Jacqueline. You better maybe wait a week, maybe two, she is not happy about this."

"Your daughter," said Madelaine, "is very stubborn, very stubborn. She is like you maybe."

"I be gone some anyway," said Du Pré.

"So where are you going?" said Madelaine.

"Brush races," said Du Pré.

"Bullshit," said Madelaine. "You are too old lose money on horse races, Du Pré. It is maybe something else, yes?"

"My Auntie Pauline," said Du Pré. "She shows up here, her husband is gone, he is in jail, does something get out of jail and is found dead."

"Poor Auntie Pauline," said Madelaine. "This is eighth, maybe tenth husband?"

"Not that many maybe," said Du Pré.

"She is crazy," said Madelaine. "But me, I like her. I call her, you got a telephone?"

Du Pré fished the number out of his wallet.

"How is Pallas?" said Du Pré.

"Scaring them here," said Madelaine. "Little shit is having a good time. They have a nice place for the kids, very nice, take good care of them, got places for the parents, too, they want to stay."

"She likes it," said Du Pré.

He looked out of the window toward the road.

Booger Tom was walking back up the road, keeping pace with a battered old pickup truck driven by someone in a cowboy hat. The truck was muddy and had Montana plates.

"I got to go," said Madelaine. "So you still love me?"

"Yah," said Du Pré.

"Good," said Madelaine. "Bye."

She hung up.

CHAPTER

8

"Like muh teeth?" said Ripper. He grinned. His front teeth were stained and ragged, one broken off to a point.

Charles Van Dusen, Du Pré thought, rich snot works for Harvey . . . good guy though . . . Pallas hunt him down like a dog . . .

"I hope," said Booger Tom, "you didn't pay yer dentist yet."

"Was in a bit of trouble," said Ripper. "Slug took them out. Missed my lips, though, damndest thing, so I had these put in. Think Pallas will like them?"

"That little brat has you in her sights," said Booger Tom. "I was you I'd run like a striped-ass ape."

"I'm here, ain't I?" said Ripper.

He grinned again, showing his awful teeth.

They went into the house and to the kitchen, Ripper carrying a soiled and battered canvas briefcase. He pulled out three envelopes and he handed one to Du Pré and one to Booger Tom and he kept one.

"Driver's licenses, insurance cards, a few receipts, and the sons of bitches didn't stick any cash in. Jesus, what assholes. They spend millions on this stuff but not one cent for the poor bastards have to carry them."

Booger Tom looked at his license.

"I think I might be gettin' old," he said. "Yes, I do."

"How likely is it someone will recognize you?" said Ripper, looking at the old cowboy.

Booger Tom shrugged.

"It ain't like I never took no summer name before," he said. "I was you, I'd worry about Du Pré, him being a famous fiddler and all."

"These folks don't like anything beautiful," said Ripper.

"Them Métis are gamblers," said Booger Tom. "I'd not fret about that. What I am in a state of wondering about is just who do you plan to ride the horse?"

Ripper nodded. He looked at Du Pré.

Du Pré rolled a smoke. "So," he said. "The races, they are not so dangerous, that I am not worried about. It is before and after. So, me, I will not ask Jacqueline about Lourdes. She will say no, load a shotgun, unless she knows that Lourdes is safe."

"That little lady rides better'n anyone I ever seen," said Booger Tom. "And thing about these here quarter-horse races is they are short, you don't got bets changing all the time, the jockeys just run them horses flat out, and that's all."

"We could bring in someone," said Ripper.

"FBI," said Du Pré, "they gots lots of jockeys, whole department of them, I know."

Ripper looked like he was about to sneeze.

"We have a guy in federal prison," said Ripper. "He's a jockey, good one, too, and we could get him out."

"Harvey, he leaves this up to us," said Du Pré, looking at Booger Tom. "This is important."

Ripper nodded.

"Guy is let out," said Du Pré, "this FBI Harvey is after, he will know."

"Yup," said Ripper.

Du Pré sighed.

"Lourdes, she is so pissed off Pallas is in Baltimore, having fun," said Du Pré. "Maybe this is good, she gets to ride, miss school some, she does better the rest of the time."

"We have to fly by ourselves at the races," said Ripper. "But there will be two teams right nearby, the moment we leave the race, and all of the way back here."

"Get rid of them," said Du Pré. "They would not help time enough."

Ripper shrugged.

"OK," said Du Pré. "I go and see."

He got in his old cruiser and he drove toward Toussaint and through it and to the house he had lived in with Catfoot and his mother and now Jacqueline and Raymond and their big brood.

It was a Saturday, and half of Du Pré's grandchildren were raising hell in the yard and the pasture beyond. They were playing Indians on real horses.

Lourdes snatched the flag from the ground where it had been dropped and she forked her legs over the saddle again and she put her face in the horse's mane and she moved away so rapidly from the other kids in pursuit that they all stopped. Her mount was the best. The gelding sailed over the fence and then they were gone down in a gully, and then up and over, Lourdes now standing in the stirrups holding the flag in her right hand.

Du Pré laughed.

Jacqueline was doing laundry, as she did every day. With twelve kids and a husband working, there was always a huge pile. Eleven kids, now.

The room in the addition Du Pré and Raymond had built was steamy and smelled of soap and bleach.

Du Pré banged on the doorjamb loudly so he wouldn't startle his daughter.

"Papa," said Jacqueline, smiling. "We will have coffee. Any of my kids break their necks yet?" And she laughed.

Twelve kids, she looks about like she did before she had any, Du Pré thought. I have two beautiful daughters . . .

They went to the kitchen.

Catfoot and his friends used to play poker at the kitchen table, for more money than their wives liked them to play for.

Jacqueline poured two cups of coffee and she brought them and they sat down.

"What you want?" said Jacqueline. "You got that line, run up and down your forehead."

Du Pré laughed.

"I need Lourdes, ride in some brush races," said Du Pré.

"Sure," said Jacqueline. "She is so pissed off, maybe she will be better then."

Du Pré looked out the window.

"These will be big money races," said Du Pré. "She maybe is gone a few days, here and there."

"OK," said Jacqueline.

"It is maybe dangerous some," said Du Pré.

Jacqueline looked at Du Pré for a long time. Then she reached over and she patted his hand.

"Life, it is dangerous," she said. "Lourdes, she is so pissed off about Pallas she rides like she is crazy. Now maybe she have something to do, it is better. She will be fourteen three months. Papa, you would not let her get hurt, I would not, but her, she is looking for it some . . ."

"It is OK then," said Du Pré.

Jacqueline looked at her father a long time.

"Madelaine call, she talk, we talk, she had talked with that Harvey," said Jacqueline. "So it is all right."

Du Pré laughed.

. . . my women they are always ahead of me . . . I think the road is empty they are just out of sight over the horizon . . .

"Bad time," said Jacqueline. "Very bad time."

Du Pré nodded.

"So," said Jacqueline, "go find your granddaughter, see she will do it. Maybe she wants, stay always in school, make those funny things pull sentences apart on."

Du Pré laughed.

He went out the back door to the pasture and he climbed up on top of the gate and he waved at Lourdes, his hat in his hand, and she saw him and set her horse at the fence and soon she had ridden up to her grandfather.

"We need a jockey, brush races," said Du Pré.

"OK," said Lourdes. "I get my things."

"*Non,*" said Du Pré. "We got to go get the horses first."

"I am going with you to get my horse I am riding," said Lourdes. "Or maybe you ride that horse yourself."

Du Pré threw up his hands.

CHAPTER

9

The man with the three horses was waiting in Sunburst. He was leading one around on a rope.

The horse was a tall gelding with a deep chest and a look of great power held in. He danced rather than walked. He was a rare color, a blue roan.

"Son of a bitch," said Booger Tom. "That is one horse, oh, yes."

They got out of the big SUV and the three of them walked over to the man who was walking the splendid horse.

"Two more in the trailer," said the man. "I will unload them."

Lourdes stepped forward, looking carefully at the big horse, and she took the rope and then she held out her hand and the horse put his lips to her palm. She moved closer and she stroked his neck. He arched his back a little and then he settled down.

Lourdes suddenly leaped up and she swung her leg over the horse's back. He turned his head to look at her.

The man who had brought the horses came out of the trailer with another lovely mount. He stopped and stared at Lourdes.

"Jesus," he said. "Usually he's hell to mount the first time till he knows who you are."

Lourdes leaned forward and she scratched the horse between his eyes.

"What is his name?" she said.

"Stewball," said the man. "Like the old song, you know, the horse who never drank water, who only drank wine . . ."

Du Pré laughed.

"Stewball was a racehorse," sang Lourdes, "and I wish he were mine . . ." Them songs, Du Pré thought, they run around the world.

"All Australian?" said Booger Tom.

The man nodded.

"One Commonwealth country to another," said the man. "Pretty easy to ship, and I was told Mr. Du Pré is a brand inspector here."

He handed some forms to Du Pré.

Du Pré nodded. He took the pen the man offered and he signed the forms and put down his badge number.

They loaded all three horses in the trailer that Du Pré had hitched to the big green SUV that morning, and the man who had brought the horses down from Canada waved once as they drove away.

They stopped halfway back to Toussaint to check the horses.

"I am going to ride, the trailer, with Stewball," said Lourdes. "We can talk."

Du Pré laughed. Lourdes opened the front access door and she got in and the horses stamped their feet a little at the intrusion.

Du Pré and Booger Tom rolled smokes before Du Pré put the big SUV in gear, and it was a few minutes before either of them spoke.

"We got a horse and a rider," said Booger Tom.

They both laughed.

"That kid was always about half spooky," said Booger Tom. "You remember the day she went out into the pasture when they had that black Arabian bastard stallion there?"

Du Pré laughed.

The stallion was fast and mean as hell, brought for breeding, and he had never been ridden. His former owner had tried and the horse had killed him. Morgan Martin, queen of the giant Martin ranch, had bought the stallion and he was in a pasture that had very tall fences, one built for very troublesome horses.

Jacqueline and Lourdes and a couple of her other kids were there for a party for a little girl, daughter of one of the hands on the ranch, and Lourdes, aged two and a half, had wandered off. She slipped through the fence and she walked out into the pasture where the black Arabian stallion was.

When Jacqueline saw her, she choked.

Everyone went out to the fence.

Jacqueline was about to crawl through and get her daughter when Morgan Martin grabbed her.

"No," she said. "Don't spook him. Look."

The black horse was standing over the tiny child, his nose in her face, and Lourdes petted his nose. Then the little girl turned and walked back to the crowd at the fence, with the mean Arabian following her, gentle as a dog. The moment the tiny girl slipped through the fence the horse reared and neighed and then he ran the circle of the fence, faster and faster.

"Damn you!" said Jacqueline to little Lourdes. "You maybe get killed."

The child just looked grave and then she slowly shook her head.

"That Arabian," said Du Pré.

"I heard the story," said Booger Tom. "I wasn't there."

"Me, either," said Du Pré.

"It don't happen very often," said Booger Tom, "but it does sometimes."

They crested a hill and saw a long road sloping down slowly to a green creek bank at the bottom, and then a long road up to the next crest.

Very big country.

"We will keep these two out to Bart's," said Booger Tom. "I think Lourdes will likely sleep with old Stewball, there."

Du Pré laughed.

"He maybe don't run, though," said Booger Tom. "I seen horses looked that good couldn't run for shit."

"Maybe," said Du Pré.

A bald eagle feeding on a road-killed deer rose up a few feet as they passed and then settled down again.

"Who's gonna shoe them?" said Booger Tom. "I'm too damn old."

"Me," said Du Pré.

"What you know about racing shoes?" said Booger Tom.

"They are some lighter," said Du Pré. "These short runs, I don't think him need weights, probably don't have an off foot anyway."

"I'd like a bit more bone in him," said Booger Tom.

"Cow horse," said Du Pré, "is not a racehorse."

They crested a long hill and saw the Wolf Mountains in the distance. The peaks were still white, even in August.

At Bart's they unloaded the three horses and put them in a big pasture that had a round corral at one end. The other horses the ranch owned were over a fence, and they bunched and ran round, excited to have visitors.

Lourdes sat on the top rail of the round corral, watching Stewball. The horse came to her, snuffling. She scratched him between his eyes.

"Who owns this horse," said Lourdes.

"Don't know," said Du Pré. "Him come from Australia."

Lourdes nodded.

"I keep him, Grandpapa," she said. "That is the deal."

"I will tell Harvey," said Du Pré.

"Him always been my horse," said Lourdes. "Him, take a while find me."

"Yah," said Du Pré.

"I expect," said Booger Tom, "that horse is worth some money." Du Pré nodded.

"Horse thief there don't care," he said. He grinned at Lourdes.

"I see that," said Booger Tom.

Ripper drove up in the old pickup and he got out. He was dressed like a ranch hand, right down to duct tape around one boot. The sole had split.

"Lourdes keeps the horse," said Booger Tom.

"That," said Ripper, "is only just."

"We maybe wrap his fetlocks," said Du Pré.

"I still wonder about them shoes," said Booger Tom.

"Do I get the notion," said Ripper, "that you two don't really know what it is you are supposed to do here?"

"That's about it," said Booger Tom.

"We don't have to," said Du Pré. "Lourdes, she knows."

CHAPTER

10

"Badger was your basic dumb shit small-time asshole," said Harvey. "He ran little packages across the border for a few bucks. You know how it is along the Canadian border."

"Yah," said Du Pré.

"When he got popped, of course he was eager to be helpful so he would not spend so very long in the slam. He didn't have anything to give us, really, about who he was carrying the Canadian blue Valium for. Badger was not the sort of fellow that one would want to trust with any information of any kind. He never saw who brought the package, never saw who picked it up, and the money was paid in cash mailed to Badger's PO box. Now, your aunt was fond of him, but no one else seems to have been. He was pretty useless."

Du Pré waited.

"But," said Harvey, "darned if old Badger there, while he sneaks over the border on some goat path, driving his Land Rover, darned if old Badger doesn't come upon a brush race. Right there on one of the Blackmore ranches. They own eleven in the West. Been around since the 1870s. Very big money, most of it in Texas, but they own three in Montana and one in Wyoming and a couple in Nebraska."

"OK," said Du Pré. "But this Badger, he is not invited and he don't got no horse or money."

"No," said Harvey. "But darned if he doesn't know one of the hands. Another idiot, useful for simple and repetitive tasks, named Fred Hahn. Fred has been known to carry stuff once in a while, too. So Fred convinces the betting folk not to stick poor Badger in a hole someplace, Badger being an old chum from way back, and further, that Badger goes deaf and dumb and blind when he is told to, so they let Badger go on his merry way, and not eight hours later Badger is up against the wall, listening to his rights, and rummaging through his tiny mind for something to offer. Which he does. And in which we are interested. Very interested."

"You are now busting gamblers?" said Du Pré. "Rich people racing horses?"

"Some of those rich people," said Harvey, "have very odd politics. They think they would be richer if the damned Jews and spics and niggers didn't conspire to tax them to death, and they think they are true patriots who must save America. For instance, us dedicated public servants here at the FBI all are agents of that selfsame International Jewish Conspiracy to take all their money and their blood for Passover matzoh."

"Oh," said Du Pré.

"People who make a whole lot of money," said Harvey, "are usually pretty smart, though limited, because they only want to make a whole lot of money, and after they make a whole lot of money they want to keep it, and keep it for their heirs and descendants, who generally are fucking morons who can't do anything in life anyway and each generation gets dimmer and dimmer."

"But it still does not make sense you are bothering with them," said Du Pré.

"Bad people a lot smarter than they are are using them to bring in dirty money, drugs, and weapons," said Harvey. "Some very bad weapons, we think . . . Now, the silly and paranoid rich, not being too very bright, think they are saving America from the et cetera."

"Shit," said Du Pré.

"So Badger gets sent off, and reasonably enough he places his paltry quarter mil on a race and claims it is money from his very best friends, which Fred Hahn tells all it must be, and Badger, not being your natural handicapper, loses it all, and since it is counterfeit, bells and whistles go off and Badger is soon lying in the sagebrush with a neat hole in his head . . ."

"Him maybe talk," said Du Pré.

"Don't think they had long enough," said Harvey. "We have a few bits of info, and far as we can tell, Badger was killed not more than a quarter hour after the race. So somebody found the bad bills, and they killed him just like that, and then they went back to reading the Protocols of the Elders of Zion. Way it looks, there weren't any of the bad smart people there, just the idiots with the horses and the big bags of cash. Kind of folks we are really after have more to do than bet money on which hunk of dog meat runs fastest."

"Who am I playing with?" said Du Pré.

"Just the idiot rich," said Harvey. "We get them but good, they will help us with the others. But we frankly lack agents of your caliber and the wonderful Booger Tom. How is the old bastard?"

Du Pré looked out of the window. Lourdes was riding Stewball flat out and the old cowboy was filming her and the horse with a video camera.

"Making movies," said Du Pré.

"Ripper's there to pull the chicken switch if things get ugly," said Harvey. "And we won't be far off."

"How dangerous," said Du Pré, "is this? My fourteen-year-old granddaughter cannot get hurt."

"I talked with Madelaine," said Harvey, "and she talked with Jacqueline, and I'd druther send those two warrior women than you two wimps, but they both know and they both said the same thing. We are in a war and though America has been less than good to the Métis, it is still the only country they happen to have."

"OK," said Du Pré.

"The jockeys are mostly Mexican kids from the ranches," said Harvey. "Riding for the jefe. And, you will be glad to know, there are a couple other girls, about Lourdes' age. Girls ride well, better than boys I am told."

Du Pré laughed.

"One of the girls is a Blackmore," said Harvey. "Anne-Marie Schroeder. Her mother is the daughter of Ferris Blackmore."

"OK," said Du Pré. "I am not so very worried now."

"All you have to do now," said Harvey, "is find a race and enter it and lay a lot of money down."

"OK," said Du Pré.

"What they do, and you probably know this, is they have a plane up and out about fifteen miles, and if the pilot sees anything, he says so and they hide the money since running horses around in the sagebrush isn't illegal yet. We can't get there fast enough unless the pilot totally fucks up, or if we have someone who keeps track of the dough and where it may fly to."

"Right," said Du Pré.

"It's simple," said Harvey. "You know, there was talk of just throwing a cordon around the race, when we found it, and searching all the vehicles that were in that circle, but we could not get a warrant. One thing they do not do is talk about these races on phones. All courier stuff. The only illegal thing they are doing is betting on the race. The race isn't by itself illegal. If we don't have recordings or movies or the money, we don't have fuck-all."

"How long you been trying this?" said Du Pré.

"Without much urgency," said Harvey, "Treasury and the IRS for twenty long years. After we picked up some chatter about some of these people and who they thought they might help out and after nine-eleven we got a lot more interested. But it is hard to crack. An illegal casino has tables and wheels and stuff. This has dog meat and a couple of suitcases and a lot of money, but connecting it all, well . . ."

"OK," said Du Pré.

"Planes flew into the World Trade Center were piloted by Israeli agents," said Harvey. "And to say that Adolf Hitler murdered six million Jews is slander on that good man's memory."

"OK," said Du Pré.

"I didn't want this," said Harvey.

"Yeah," said Du Pré, "you did."

"Everybody in the world would play nice," said Harvey, "I could retire and go fishing."

"You hate to fish," said Du Pré.

"Smelly things," said Harvey. "Slimy, too."

"There isn't any place left that is out of the way," said Du Pré. "Not even Montana, few people, whole lot of not much next to a whole lot of nothing."

"No," said Harvey, "there isn't any place."

"Yah," said Du Pré.

CHAPTER

11

Du Pré opened the letter from Canada. Auntie Pauline's telephone bills and a note.

He looked at the bills. Four collect calls. The number for each of those was the same. Du Pré went to the telephone book. The calls Badger had placed had come from Minneapolis.

Du Pré put the bills in another envelope and he addressed it to Harvey and he put on two stamps just to be sure and he went out and down the street to the post office, a tiny block building with a flag flapping out in front.

"Du Pré," said Ellen Pritchett, postmistress.

Du Pré handed her the letter and she weighed it and nodded and she canceled the stamps and she put it in the bin.

"Go out tomorrow," she said. "Heard from Madelaine and Pallas?"

"Yah," said Du Pré. "Madelaine is having Pallas measured, a cage. Soon as it is welded shut with her in it she come home, yes."

Ellen laughed.

"Your family," she said, "has a lot of very bright people in it."

"Me," said Du Pré, "the exception, you know."

"Right," said Ellen. "You are tone-deaf, too."

Du Pré went back out and he walked up the street past the little Catholic church where Father Van Den Heuvel tended his flock and they him. The big priest was so clumsy he had knocked himself out a few times by shutting his head in the door of his car. He was pruning the lilacs.

Big piles of small twigs lay here and there near the bushes.

"Late for that," said Du Pré.

"I know," said Father Van Den Heuvel, "I—," and he let out a howl. Du Pré went to him. He had sliced his finger open with the loppers.

"How you do that?" said Du Pré. Cutting a finger in loppers with long handles was a near-impossible task.

"I have a gift," said Father Van Den Heuvel, wrapping a kerchief around his finger. Blood soon seeped through it.

"That will need stitches," said Du Pré.

"Nonsense," said Father Van Den Heuvel. Then he got very pale and he fainted dead away.

Du Pré got his old cruiser and he cursed some while he heaved the priest into the backseat and then he took off toward the clinic in Cooper. Father Van Den Heuvel rose up in the rearview mirror.

"I will be all right," he said, collapsing again.

Du Pré pulled up to the little clinic and he went in.

"I got the priest again," he said to the nurse.

She nodded. She fetched a wheelchair and they went out and helped the good father into it.

"I have to go that way after work," said the nurse. "I'll drop him off."

Father Van Den Heuvel straightened up in the wheelchair,

looked at the bloody kerchief his hand was wrapped in, and passed out again.

The nurse pulled the chair backward through the clinic doors.

Du Pré shook his head and he got in his cruiser and he roared off. He headed toward Bart's place, west and north of Toussaint.

Booger Tom and Lourdes were at work on the track.

Lourdes bent over the horse's neck as she rode, rider and horse pounding down the track. Like all good riders, she was part of her mount.

The horse floated under her, and Lourdes did not move at all.

Booger Tom looked at the stopwatch.

"That," he said, "is some horse. Ol' noble Stewball. Them old songs is so old, you say, I wonder what it was about 'fore the horse rode into it."

"Maybe it is always about horses," said Du Pré. "People racing on them for a long time."

"Bettin' on them, too," said Booger Tom. "Well, these is straight-up races so we don't got to watch a tote board. Not that I ever seen one of them."

Du Pré laughed.

"Blackmore is what we is after, I guess," said Booger Tom. "I done worked for his father a long time ago. Good feller, he was."

Du Pré looked at the old cowboy.

"Killed his wife," said Booger Tom. "They was a-fightin' and he busted her neck. But he had enough money so no one kicked up any dust. Put her out in the corral and said she'd fallen off a horse and that passed, but we all knew. I left about then. Thing of it was, old Blackmore blamed hisself so bad he stuck a gun in his mouth not that long after. Three kids, Ferris the oldest, time he was old enough to take over—had to be thirty, accordin' to the will—he'd done three tours in Veet Nam. Officer, of course. He liked it, I hear."

Du Pré looked at the old cowboy.

"You have been talking to people," said Du Pré.

"Gonna stick yer head in the grizzly's mouth," said Booger Tom, "it is good to know what manner of bear he be."

"So," said Du Pré.

"He come back from that war," said Booger Tom, "about crazy. Hated the Commies and then he takes over the Blackmore ranches. Took him a long time find a woman crazy enough to marry him, so he's in his sixties now and his granddaughter's fourteen and Daddy ain't mellowed none."

Du Pré nodded.

"Wal," said Booger Tom, "he's richer than the Devil's mistress and been puttin' money into all sorts of dingy political things, keeps his name buried. He was a lot of the dough behind all them magazines sprung up spent their time writing about the Clintons and how they made their dough running dope. Now, I never actually spoke to the man, just seen him a few times. He's crazier than a shithouse rat and rich enough so's he don't get stuck in the bug bin for it."

Du Pré nodded.

"You recall when the FBI and about every other federal cop was all over Montana looking for them planes was stolen? Them two P-38s? Twin-boom Lightnings. I seen them when I was fighting the Krauts. Fearsome they was. Carried eight Browning fifties and four twenty-millimeter cannons. Some was sold as surplus after the war, but the ones the feds was after had been stole with all the guns on 'em. Never found squat."

Du Pré looked at Booger Tom.

"If they is here in Montana," the old cowboy said, "they'd likely be on one of the Blackmore spreads. Underground hangar. Blackmore's a pilot, too."

"So," said Du Pré, "you are saying watch out some."

"Yeah," said Booger Tom. "You watch out a lot."

"He is dangerous," said Du Pré.

"They all are," said Booger Tom. "You know them old boys, own them big spreads. They live like they was lords a thousand years ago."

Du Pré nodded.

"So here we are," said Booger Tom, "the sport of kings, that is, if you don't count makin' war."

"And he could if he wanted," said Du Pré.

"Twin-boom Lightning," said Booger Tom. "We was fightin' in the Huertgen Forest, seen one of them dive, strafe something a couple miles away. We took another day to get there. Know what we found? About forty trucks and light tanks and about four hundred dead Krauts. Just that one plane, took it about one minute. See, the pilot had her guns all goin' and he made two passes and was gone. Unloaded every slug he had. Cut trucks in half, hit some fuel drums with the cannon rounds and they blew, but I never forgot it, just that one plane."

"Jesus," said Du Pré.

"We go in there and leave the money and we hold our mouths just right," said Booger Tom. "Just exactly right. They all think the government is after them personal-like and they all are *pre*pared go out in glory."

Du Pré shook his head.

"Me," he said, "I don't want take Lourdes there."

"Then we can't do nothin'," said Booger Tom. "Can't do a damn thing without a rider, jockey, whatever."

"Why you quit Blackmore?" said Du Pré.

"Same reason I quit everybody," said Booger Tom. "One fine day it is time to move on."

CHAPTER

12

Lourdes and Stewball shot past, the tall horse reaching for every foot of ground. Booger Tom pressed the stem of the stopwatch and he grinned hugely.

"We got a horse and we got a rider," he said, "and soon as we can get us some chickens to pluck, we got feathers, too."

"That is some horse," said Du Pré. "Me, I would not know what to do with a horse that is that good."

"Bet on him heavy," said Booger Tom, "is what you do. Now, you never been to one of these high-dollar brush races?"

Du Pré shook his head.

"Catfoot and some of his friends would race, Fourth of July," said Du Pré, "maybe bet a hundred dollars."

"Wal," said Booger Tom, "I expect the company we are seekin' thinks a hundred grand is nothin' to mind. Way they run these races is pretty fair on the face of it. Feller hostin' it can't enter no horse. All the other horses has had to travel, would give the host's horse an advantage. Since he don't have an interest in the race directly, he holds the money and makes the pays. Simple. Provides the plane and the lookout."

Du Pré nodded.

"Wintertime they have cockfights and dogfights. Them Mexican dogs got heads like beartraps," said Booger Tom. "Bettin' fellers will bet on how many flies land on a pile of shit in the next two minutes."

Du Pré nodded.

Catfoot would bet on pretty much anything. Mama Du Pré first prayed that he would quit, and after that seemed most unlikely she lit candles to saints praying he would win.

"Your Pa would bet some," said Booger Tom. "I used to consider him a regular sort of income till he threatened to shoot me if I showed up at the poker game again."

"Catfoot," said Du Pré, "him, he get some upset about them cards."

"Numbers," said Booger Tom, "was not his strong suit. He thought the odds was somethin' you could beat. It is a fairly common and always fatal belief."

Lourdes had slowed Stewball and the big horse was loping along now, shaking his head.

"He likes runnin' fast," said Booger Tom. "That horse has a proud heart. Lots of horses will run, but that proud heart will make him win more."

Du Pré nodded.

"Blue roan, too," said Booger Tom. "With that pale mane and tail, be hell to paint him up, make him look like another horse."

"You ever have an honest thought?" said Du Pré.

Booger Tom looked hurt.

"That's a hell of a thing to say," he said. "Some folks go past a church and mutter them a prayer; I can't pass a bank without eyein' it for one of them sudden unexpected withdrawals."

Du Pré laughed.

"Goddamned country went to hell when they quit carryin' the big money on trains," said Booger Tom. "Used to be a young feller could get a start in life by robbin' a train, or a few if he had big plans, and then go to honest work if he could stand it."

Lourdes came up to them, Stewball dancing on his feet. The big horse fuffled and tossed his head. Du Pré stroked his pround arched neck.

"All my life," said Lourdes, "I dream of this horse. I see him plenty. See him running on the tall grass when the dew is coming off in the morning and there are clouds on the ground."

She grinned.

"I hope you know how much Bart paid for that nag," said Booger Tom.

"I don't care," said Lourdes. "He is mine."

"Missy," said Booger Tom, "we are goin' to do some serious business and I may ask you to lose a race or two."

"Ask me all that you want," said Lourdes. "Stewball here, he will not run to lose, you know."

"Missy," said Booger Tom, "this is important."

"Stewball, me, we talk about it," said Lourdes, "let you know."

She laughed then and turned the big blue roan and she whistled and he leaped forward and soon they were flying over the pasture grass. Stewball came to the back fence and he cleared it by six feet.

"Things could be worse," said Du Pré. "We could have Pallas."

Booger Tom shuddered.

A battered pickup with fencing tools and a few rolls of wire and two shovels in the bed sockets came in the gate. Booger Tom looked at the truck.

It came closer.

"I don't know that truck," said Booger Tom.

Du Pré shrugged.

The truck pulled up and the driver got out. His hat was pulled way down and he had a kerchief on the bottom half of his face.

He tugged at the kerchief when he got close.

"Like muh new rig?" said Ripper. He smiled with his awful teeth.

"I take it," said Booger Tom, "you are tryin' to blend in."

"I am blending in," said Ripper.

Booger Tom nodded.

"Ya walk like you got a poker up yer ass," he said. "Spot you for a dude a mile away."

Ripper nodded.

"Anything else?" he said.

"If you try to be some feller you ain't," said Booger Tom, "you will stick out like a turd in the punchbowl. What ya got to remember is that there is about three hundred million folks in America two hundred million of which is dreamin' of becomin' cowboys. Cowboys is the highest evolved form of human life, of course, and so there is people sort of sneakin' out here from real unlikely places to try their luck at higher evolution. They got a real slim chance of makin' the grade and you are so sorry you got none at all but we do give points for wishful thinkin', no matter how pathetic the feller is doin' it. Now, I known you a while but I got no idea where you call home, other'n it has to be one of them hellholes out east everybody lives in."

"Virginia," said Ripper. "Arlington."

"Nice try," said Booger Tom. "You mean to tell me you done growed up in Washington, D.C., where the worst criminals in America spend all their time annoying people like me."

"God-*danged* guvverment," said Ripper.

"You see how a feller would get cranky about folks paid out of his taxes spend all their time dreamin' up new ways to piss ya off," said Booger Tom.

"There is a point to this lecture," said Ripper. "I have faith. Even such a splendid example of crusty old Western Farthood should surely have a fucking *point* to all this gas he is emitting," said Ripper.

"Point is," said Booger Tom, "we got all sorts of outlaws here used to be bankers and stockbrokers and busyness ex-ek-u-tives and college professors and other sorts of shit jobs finally tossed it all over and come to be cowboys. So you don't need to paint yerself over that much. Lots of folks out here stompin' through the cowshit used to be the very cream of society."

"All right," said Ripper. "How 'bout I just tell them I used to be an FBI agent but I repented."

"I would not," said Booger Tom, "mention it I was you. You do anything sides steal hubcaps and knock up the neighbor girls 'fore you went to the FBI?"

"I majored in English literature," said Ripper.

"Son," said Booger Tom, "you done come to the right place."

CHAPTER

13

Du Pré saw the man in the white hat at the gate, and he swung the gate open and Du Pré crawled through, the heavy horse trailer jerking as it crossed the cattle guard. The gate was swung shut. Du Pré rolled down his window. He saw a gleam behind a huge rock that stuck up out of the land, just a brief shimmer. A gun.

Booger Tom opened the other door and he got out.

Somebody shone a light on the old man's face and then it flashed to Du Pré. Quick, and gone.

"I'm Dave Wilson," said the old cowboy.

"Where's the jockey?" said a voice.

"In the trailer with her horse," said Booger Tom.

A light played in the trailer, a man walked down one side and around the end and up toward to Du Pré.

"About ten miles on," said the voice.

Booger Tom got back in and Du Pré eased the truck forward. The headlights picked up tire tracks, many of them.

"So," said Booger Tom, "first race she does flat out."

Du Pré grunted.

There were two pistols in the pockets of the doors. All people who carried horses carried them. A horse could be injured badly enough to have to be shot. Du Pré had his .270 in the gun rack behind his head.

"This first time won't amount to nothin'," said Booger Tom. "It's the next one and the ones after that."

"Yah," said Du Pré.

They went up and over a hill and down a winding switchback to a small creek thickly banked with cottonwoods. Their sweet scent filled the air.

The road went on along the creek for five miles and then turned to the right and went up a long sloping rise.

At the top of the hill they could see down into a huge flat bowl, and there were many lights there out in the middle.

They drove slowly up to the mass of trucks and trailers.

A small airplane droned overhead and passed to the east, lights blinking on wings and tail.

Du Pré parked where a man with a flashlight pointed.

They got out and opened the back of the trailer and Lourdes backed Stewball out. The big horse whinnied, and other horses answered.

Lourdes pulled the halter and the blue roan followed her. She walked him in a wide circle.

There was a faint thin line of pink across the eastern horizon.

"Light enough in an hour," said Booger Tom. "We'll run and be gone 'fore most folks wake up."

Lourdes walked Stewball for fifteen minutes and then she came back and Booger Tom and Du Pré helped her put on the little saddle and the headstall and thin reins.

Stewball tossed his head and he snorted.

"To the line!" came a loud, deep voice.

Nine portable stock gates had been set to make eight bays for the starting line. There was a finish a quarter mile away, two poles, and a couple of men with a camera on a tripod.

Booger Tom wandered over to a big man in rumpled clothes who wore a feed company logo on his baseball cap. The man stood behind a cheap folding table.

Booger Tom waited while two men in front of him set down bundles of cash. Then he spoke to the big rumpled man and he put down some.

Other men came, bet, and retreated quickly.

Lourdes led Stewball to the bays, and a cowboy looked at her and he whooped.

"That's Ferris Blackmore," said Booger Tom. "I look some different, he didn't twitch or look twice."

Blackmore was a big white-haired man in a gabardine western suit.

Du Pré nodded.

Lourdes got up on Stewball, limber as a monkey climbing a tree, and she settled herself. Stewball stood absolutely still while the other seven horses were brought up, all of them whickering and dancing and eyeing their neighbors.

Some of the other bettors looked at Lourdes and her stone-still mount and whispered.

"Two minutes," called Ferris Blackmore. He had walked from the table to the starting bays, and he held a small pistol in his hand.

"Think they was a bunch of sprinters," said Booger Tom. "Horses don't generally like loud noises, but then they don't like waving flags, neither. We done made a good impression already. All the rest of that dogmeat is screwing around. Stewball has his eye on that finish line and nothin' else. We will be some richer soon enough."

Du Pré rolled a smoke and he lit it. He nodded.

Booger Tom grinned.

The other riders were mounted finally, and in the bay to the right of Lourdes and Stewball there was another girl, one taller than Lourdes, thin as a whip, with bright gold hair tied up. She looked at Lourdes and Lourdes looked at her and they locked eyes for a time and then both looked forward.

"That's the Schroeder gal," said Booger Tom. "Her mount's a bit antsy."

Ferris Blackmore raised the little pistol, pointing it straight up, looking at his watch, and the gun popped and the horses all leaped forward, but Stewball had half a length on all the others right out of the gate.

The blue roan headed for the finish, and he pulled ahead even more, and the race was so short that it was over before Du Pré had taken another drag on his smoke.

The camera flashed at the finish and the riders began to slow their mounts. All but Lourdes. Stewball wanted to run, damn it, and so he did, rising up the hill beyond like he had wings, and Lourdes turned him at the top and they raced back down and wide of the knot of men around Ferris Blackmore and the money.

All eyes were on the blue roan as he passed.

Lourdes jumped down near Du Pré and she began to lead Stewball around in a fast walk, then slowed him down to cool him after his run. The big horse was sweating a little, just a little.

Booger Tom ambled back, one pocket of his leather jacket bulging.

Ferris Blackmore and another man came soon.

"I won't sell him," said Booger Tom.

"Damn shame ya cut him," said Blackmore.

"Cut 'fore I found him," said Booger Tom. "He was a-pullin' a vegetable wagon in Sydney—"

"Australian," said Blackmore. There was no question in the word.

"Yup," said Booger Tom.

"Fine horse," said Blackmore. "Rider's good, too. Who is she?"

"His granddaughter," said Booger Tom. "Frenchy Injun gal."

Blackmore nodded.

"Anne-Marie would like to meet her," said Blackmore.

The girl with the gold hair came slowly behind her grandfather, her hands working on each other as she looked at the ground.

Lourdes was still cooling Stewball off.

They waited until she walked the roan to the trailer. Du Pré took the reins and he slipped off the headstall and saddle and the big blue roan just climbed in the trailer without complaint.

"This is Anne-Marie," said Blackmore, his hand on the girl's shoulder.

"Lourdes," said Booger Tom. "Lourdes St. Vrain."

The two girls stared at each other again.

Then they shook hands very formally.

Anne-Marie turned on her heel and walked back toward her horse.

CHAPTER 14

Jacqueline stepped up on the rail fence. She put a hand over her eyes and she peered out toward the foothills that leaned against the Wolf Mountains.

Lourdes and Stewball were floating over the grassy land.

"She, that horse, they like each other some," said Du Pré.

"I been around horses all my life," said Jacqueline, "been around Lourdes all her life. Lourdes has had a lot of horses to ride. She is gone, isn't she?"

"Yah," said Du Pré. "Turned that corner."

Jacqueline got down.

"Papa," she said, "after Mama die, you are sad, we are sad, we start getting older, Maria she raises some hell, me, I find my Raymond, I quit school, have babies. You don't give us much shit."

Du Pré laughed.

"Me," he said, "I do not know what to do, so I don't do much."

"*Non,*" said Jacqueline. "You tell us, Mama is gone, you are not God, and you help if you can. I have twelve kids now. I am worse confused than you. Pallas, she is some genius. Me, I cannot help with that. Lourdes, she is spooky. Hervé, him, want to be a cop, since he was small. They all know what to do, I guess."

Lourdes and Stewball shot down a hill and disappeared behind a fold of land. Then they appeared, suddenly much closer.

"That horse," said Jacqueline, "worth more than this little ranch here, yes?"

Du Pré nodded.

"Why don't that Bart and Booger Tom make her keep him out at Bart's? We just got that little shed for him."

"Lourdes pitch a fit," said Du Pré, "about Stewball left out there. This I expect. We drive off with Lourdes. Stewball pitch a fit. Him, he dash back about fifty feet and then, him, he clear the pole fence which is six feet high and come down the road after us, mad as hell. Me, I give up. Lourdes, she must go to school, sometimes. Stewball, him, he don't like it she is not around."

"He is a grown horse, they meet," said Jacqueline. "You would think he would be a little more grownup about it."

Du Pré laughed.

"They meet," said Du Pré, "they know each other. She rides in the trailer with him."

"School is out, Stewball knows it, jumps the fence, goes on down there. They walk home together," said Jacqueline. "You ever have a horse do that?"

"*Non,*" said Du Pré.

"Maybe I have so many kids, lose count, the fairies stick a couple in," said Jacqueline. "Me, I thought I would fetch up little Métis do ordinary stuff. Some of them will, they don't kill each other off first."

There were squalls and wails coming from the front yard.

"It is all right," said Jacqueline. "Been coming all day. They are killing the wounded now."

Howls . . . yells.

"Wounded have risen, doing battle again," said Jacqueline. "I figure this is only maybe a four-bandage one. Lots less blood since that little shit Pallas left. She play for keeps."

Du Pré laughed.

"Papa," said Jacqueline, "there is that Benetsee . . ."

Du Pré looked.

Lourdes and Stewball had been pounding down the hill and then across the meadow and Benetsee was suddenly just there, and they circled him.

Lourdes and Stewball stopped and Lourdes slipped down. Stewball stood, then tossed his head, and Benetsee stroked his neck.

Du Pré looked at Jacqueline.

"There is trouble," said Jacqueline softly. "I know this when Madelaine call me. Now I really know it. He is like the raven flies past before the storm comes. I have not seen him two, three months."

Du Pré nodded. A small worm wriggled up his spine and a cold drop of sweat trickled down it.

"She will be all right, though," said Du Pré. "That is why he is here now."

"I thought him, Canada," said Jacqueline.

Du Pré nodded.

Lourdes got back up on Stewball and then Benetsee appeared on the horse, sitting behind her. Stewball looked back once and he shrugged and walked slowly toward Jacqueline and Du Pré.

When they got near, Benetsee slipped down, landing softly on his feet. Then he hobbled like the little old man he was.

"Du Pré, Jacqueline," said Benetsee, "it is good to see you."

He was filthy, his clothes black with soot and wear, showing greasy black at the knees.

"Old man," said Jacqueline, "you stink like a dead goat. You come, clean up, have supper. First you clean up though."

Benetsee grinned at Du Pré.

"You got to do something about your women," he said.

Du Pré shook his head.

"Like my head, my neck," he said. "You, you are on your own."

Benetsee stepped through the fence and he followed Jacqueline to the house and they went in.

"Him, something," said Lourdes, "give me this," and she held up a little medicine bag that hung round her neck on a black thong.

"Sewn shut," said Lourdes, "so I will not know what is in it."

"Yah," said Du Pré.

"Stewball don't fuss when him get on," said Lourdes. "He don't weigh much."

Du Pré nodded.

"Him say something I don't understand," said Lourdes.

"Yes," said Du Pré. "I don't ever understand him."

Not until much later, anyway.

"Him say I find a friend when I need one when I sing," said Lourdes.

"Him give you the song?" said Du Pré.

"*Non,*" said Lourdes.

Du Pré slowly rolled a smoke and he lit it and he sucked a draught deep into his lungs.

"Then you have the song already," said Du Pré.

"I got a lot of songs," said Lourdes. "Which one he mean?"

"You will know," said Du Pré. He looked off to the mountains.

"Grandpapa," said Lourdes, "those people, the race, they are pretty dangerous people I am thinking."

Du Pré nodded.

"Not many of them," said Lourdes.

"Other races there will be more," said Du Pré.

The back door of the house slammed and they turned to see Jacqueline carrying a bundle of clothes to the fire pit. She doused them with kerosene and she lit a match.

"Hee," said Lourdes. "Nepthele be missing some clothes now, you bet."

69

Jacqueline appeared with the running shoes Benetsee had worn. She had a can of spray in her hand and she soaked the shoes with the fluid.

"I am maybe going to boil that old goat," said Jacqueline. And she smiled with her perfect white teeth.

"I build the fire," said Du Pré.

CHAPTER

15

"The money was all good," said Foote over the telephone.

"OK," said Du Pré.

"So tell me about the race," said Foote. "From the take I gather it was not a big one."

"Eight horses," said Du Pré. "Very well run, they start not long after dawn, bets laid down, horses run, payoffs made, then everyone goes away."

"Blackmore didn't run a horse, though," said Foote.

"I think so," said Du Pré. "His granddaughter she rides for him. What I think, maybe, the horse she is riding was brought from another of his ranches. They all know each other, so it is all right with the others."

"Makes sense," said Foote. "I'm concerned for you and Lourdes and that old outlaw Booger Tom. If you want to pull out, Harvey won't complain."

"I will not, Lourdes will not, Booger Tom will not," said Du Pré. "It is a bad bunch of people. Sound like Nazis."

"Some of them," said Foote, "would like to have been. What they are is very, very angry and utterly ignorant. And very, very rich. They have a secret society, called the Patrick Henry Patriots. His 'Give me liberty or give me death . . .' Did you know while he made that speech his wife was chained to the wall of his basement?"

"*Non,*" said Du Pré. "Harvey, he does not tell me much."

"Harvey," said Foote, "is beside himself. One of the dingbat groups he has been after, a white supremacist movement in Texas, got warned about a raid. The warning could only have come from within the FBI. Harvey is a bit obsessed with finding out who it was."

"That bomb killed three agents," said Du Pré. "I read something about it."

"Yeah," said Foote, "that bomb, which was a certain kind of bomb. It was the sort of bomb the Palestinian terrorists make. Very sophisticated."

"Everything bad in the world is the Jews," said Du Pré.

"Yup," said Foote. "Think about it. If all of the terror groups merge, everyone from the Irish Republican Army to the home-grown Nazis to the Arab terrorists who are obsessed with destroying Israel to the cocaine lords to those countries which sponsor them, the problem gets very large indeed."

"Yah," said Du Pré. "So Harvey, he does not tell me all of this."

"Harvey," said Foote, "had to tell me before Bart would allow our help. Harvey is a good man. I think that you may take it that this is important enough for him to risk the lives of friends, one of whom is a . . . thirteen-year-old girl?"

"Yah," said Du Pré. "We had to have a rider."

"Lourdes," said Foote. "I could check her file—"

"You got files, Jacqueline's kids?" said Du Pré.

"Bart really wants to help," said Foote. "You know how he is. Your daughter has so many children it is hard for me to recall them all instanter."

"Shit," said Du Pré. "I can never remember."

"So," said Foote, "the money is on the way back. Some of it was marked, by the way. Ink, showed up with filtered ultraviolet light. Pretty complex."

"OK," said Du Pré. "I am going to fish down my machine gun that I do not have."

"I did not hear that," said Foote. "Enjoy." And he hung up.

Du Pré walked out to the barn behind Bart's house. The two other horses brought from Australia were in their stalls, eating.

Booger Tom came out of a stall with a small shovel and a bucketful of horseshit.

"Ya look like somebody buggered yer best goat," said Booger Tom.

Du Pré laughed.

"I am worried some," he said.

Booger Tom set down the bucket and shovel.

"Let's smoke," said Booger Tom. They walked outside. Du Pré rolled a smoke for himself and he handed his pouch and papers to the old cowboy, who rolled his smoke one-handed.

"Kin still do it," he said. "It don't really count cause I ain't ridin' a horse fast, but it will have to do."

"This is some dangerous," said Du Pré. "I do not like having Lourdes, she is a kid, you know."

The old cowboy nodded.

"That," he said, "bothers me a lot. But both her mother and that fine woman of yours said go ahead, and I kin guarantee you Old Stewball there will not let anyone else ride him now. I seen a couple kids know horse before, but nothin' like Lourdes. She and that gelding know each other down real deep, and they are gonna run together till he dies."

Du Pré nodded.

"I think I get down that gun of mine," he said.

"That Kraut thing?" said Booger Tom. "Me, I wouldn't mind havin' it around. Carried one all the damn way from south France to Vienna."

Du Pré looked at him.

"Seventh Army," said Booger Tom, "Truscott's army. He didn't like to blow his own horn, not like Patton and them others. Kept a loose hand on his army, though it was there when it was needed. We killed more Krauts and took more territory than anybody. We'd run over the Germans, and whatever they had, we'd use, slap a coat of olive drab on a plane or a tank or whatever, and head on. We liked them machine pistols, didn't jam up the way ours did."

Du Pré nodded.

"But I think you'd best not," said Booger Tom. "See, I think maybe not the next race but the one after that we will begin learnin' things, and you kin bet they'll go through our rig with tweezers. They'll expect the pistols."

"They are nuts like they are supposed to be," said Du Pré, "they will not be surprised they find that."

"Mebbe," said Booger Tom. "I would think they'd all have stuff get them ten years in the federal pen they get caught."

Du Pré sighed.

"Me," he said, "I would like, play my fiddle, drink good whiskey, smoke good tobacco, be with my Madelaine, watch my grandchildren grow."

Booger Tom nodded.

"These people," he said, "would just like to kill them grandchildren, and you know it, fer not bein' white enough."

Du Pré sighed.

"Yah," he said.

"I'd rather be robbin' trains," said Booger Tom. "Thing about it is the world don't seem to pay much attention to what I'd *like*."

"Yah," said Du Pré.

"Yer warrior women want us on this," said Booger Tom. "It'd be some different they didn't."

Du Pré laughed.

"I think I go see Benetsee," said Du Pré.

Booger Tom nodded.

"You do that," he said. "And I will clean and oil up your Schmeisser and see it works good."

Du Pré laughed.

"I busted into a bunker," said Booger Tom, "with one of them, found all these Kraut artillerymen having breakfast. Thirty of them. Couple of them dove for their guns, so I cut loose. Killed them all."

Du Pré nodded.

"Hell of a world we live in, ain't it?" said Booger Tom.

"It is getting worse," said Du Pré.

"Not," said Booger Tom, "if we just don't let it do that."

CHAPTER

18

Smoke rose up lazily from the fire pit behind Benetsee's little cabin. Du Pré parked his old cruiser and he walked round and down the hill. The sweat lodge was near the little creek, a long narrow pool of water handy to dive into after the heat of the sweat lodge.

Benetsee was not there. A kingfisher flew swiftly down the stream, kakking loudly, and a moment later the old man came out of the willows, his arms full of green leafy branches.

The smoke from the fire pit had thinned, and the stones lay upon white ash with hot coals under them.

"Sweat," said the old man.

Du Pré went to the piece of canvas laid on the grass near the sweat lodge and he stripped. He picked up the shovel and he lifted stones from the fire pit on the blade and he put them in the lodge, in the pit made for them near the door. Then he got in and Benetsee joined him, and the old man poured water on the stones and steam billowed up and Benetsee pulled down the flap and they sat in the wet dark while the heat reached for their bones.

It was very hot and very close.

Benetsee poured more water on the stones, which still glowed dark red, and there was a loud hiss and the air thickened more.

Du Pré breathed deep.

He closed his eyes and he lay back and Benetsee started to sing in a language Du Pré did not know but had heard many times.

He hummed with the strange words.

Another hiss.

More steam, almost thick enough to choke on.

Benetsee shouted once, and Du Pré felt the air move as though something giant had flown by right overhead, and then the old man sang again and a sweet odor filled the air, smoldering willow leaves put green on the stones.

Du Pré coughed and then he choked. He made for the door and he wriggled out and he slid into the long pool of cold water, shimmering little brook trout flashing in the waving water weeds.

He opened his eyes beneath the water and saw the sun on stones and the rippling shadows of light falling through running water.

He came up gasping. The water was icy and the change from deep heat to wet cold made him feel suddenly very much younger, the aches in his joints were gone and his muscles felt limber.

He grabbed a thin dead tree, cut off a couple feet above the ground, and he pulled himself out and he sat gasping on the grassy bank.

There was a movement in the willows across the stream and Du Pré saw a face, a big cat's, a mountain lion there looking at him with flat yellow eyes, and then the cat came forward, ears lifted, walking as though her paws were on thin ice.

Du Pré looked at the big cat.

"Go on, you," he said.

The cat backed away, turned, went into the willows, and was gone.

Du Pré waited until the wind dried him and then he went to his clothes and he dressed.

Benetsee was still in the sweat lodge, singing, and there were other voices with him, faint and seeming to be far off, though Du Pré was only eight or ten feet from the old man.

He smiled and shook his head.

Benetsee suddenly came out, swiftly, and he went belly first down the bank to the pool, sinuous as an otter.

Du Pré watched a shadow go to the foot of the pool and come back, and then the old man's head appeared and he made for the bank and Du Pré went to him and he knelt and offered a hand and Benetsee grabbed it and Du Pré hauled him out.

The old man grinned and he picked his clothes off the bush nearby, all of them new-looking.

Nepthele, him down to two pairs of jeans, Du Pré thought.

Benetsee laughed.

"You are worried," he said. "Good."

Du Pré nodded.

"Good," said Benetsee. "You remember you, you."

Du Pré laughed, and he turned away for a moment, and when he next looked at the spot where the old man had been he was not there.

Du Pré walked back up to his cruiser and he got in and backed and turned and drove out to the county road and down to Toussaint and he parked at the roadhouse.

One of the letters had fallen from the sign on the false-front second story.

TOUSSAINT SA OON it now said.

Du Pré walked east and he found the letter in the woodpile. He looked at it. The nails which had held it had rusted away.

"They all come down now," he said to himself.

Susan Klein was behind the bar looking intently at a crossword puzzle. Du Pré went behind and made himself a ditchwater highball and he drank half of it and he pulled a drawer open that hung beneath the bar toward the right end and he took out a hammer and he fished around and found three good heavy galvanized nails.

"Your sign is falling off," he said.

"Yes," said Susan. "But what is a seven-letter word meaning anti-tank weapon?"

"Bazooka," said Du Pré. "Now I go and fix your sign."

"I knew that," said Susan Klein.

"Now you do," said Du Pré. He went outside and around back and found the extension ladder and he brought it round and set it against the half roof that ran the full length of the front of the building. He climbed up and he walked across the cedar shakes, crunching, to the place the letter had fallen out of, and he nailed it back on.

Four others fell off.

"Shit," said Du Pré.

"Ain't life grand," said Ripper. He was standing out in the street, grinning, with his godawful teeth.

"Me, I need a drilldriver, screws," said Du Pré.

Ripper fished the tool and some screws out of the crossbox in the back of the old pickup and he came up the ladder nimble as a goat and Du Pré held the letters in place while Ripper put two heavy screws deep into the wood.

"Get all the others, too," said Ripper. He kept on.

"You are here why?" said Du Pré.

"I am here," said Ripper, "cause I ain't noplace else. Truth to tell, I am here fetching a few things for I have me a new job as a lowly cowboy on one of the Blackmore spreads out in South Dakota."

"Cowboy," said Du Pré, "is not what you think."

"Shitwork," said Ripper. "I know, I know, can't-see to can't-see, and mostly fixing fence. Feller like Blackmore has a lot of fence."

"Why there?" said Du Pré.

"I could get on there," said Ripper. "Also, we know the big race is there. Six weeks hence."

"Hence," said Du Pré. "You are tapping telephones."

"Why," said Ripper, "that would violate the right of privacy these demented pricks are all entitled to."

"Hence," said Du Pré.

"You got three races before," said Ripper, "but that one is the big one."

"You be careful," said Du Pré.

"Oh, yes," said Ripper. "And you, too."

CHAPTER

17

"We got an advantage," said Booger Tom. The morning was cold and the breath of the men and the horses smoked in the pale early light.

Du Pré nodded.

"Just a hundred twenty miles," said Lourdes. "Stewball he is all limber, didn't tighten up in the ride."

They were standing away from the twelve-bay starting post set in the huge pasture. A small plane droned overhead, circling a few miles out, the pilot holding the same set to his wings.

There were a hundred people there, mostly men, but a few women in expensive clothes and handmade boots in snake or ostrich leathers. One spectacularly beautiful blonde wore very tight jeans and high pale gray lizard boots and a short fur jacket that glowed richly.

"That whore's got a mink coat on," said Booger Tom, "and that is Las Vegas money. There's some big bills down on this race, and it ain't but a medium-sized bettin' day."

Lourdes checked Stewball's hooves. The big blue roan lifted one foot after another as soon as the girl touched his fetlock.

She put down the last hoof and she shivered in her down coat.

"Three to post!" said Ferris Blackmore.

Lourdes took off her coat and she handed it to Du Pré and she led Stewball toward the post. They paused in front of a man with a clipboard and he said something and pointed. Lourdes went to the bay and a cowboy swung open the gate. She went in and got up on the horse and began to check herself and the saddle and bridle.

"Cold morning," said Booger Tom. He was glowing red, the whiskey veins in his nose all swollen.

Du Pré nodded.

Anne-Marie Schroeder took a bay next to Lourdes and the two girls stared at each other without speaking, and then both looked ahead at the short track. They both began to settle in and they gathered the reins, adjusting the pull.

"Two minutes to post!" called Ferris Blackmore. He had the little pistol in his hand.

Du Pré looked round at the crowd, all of whom wore ranching clothes but the fancy women and all of whom looked silently at the twelve bays and twelve horses running.

There was one small knot of men who did not fit. They had on windbreakers and all of them were dressed in black. They wore heavy black boots with thick soles and the lacings were laddered like a paratrooper's jump gear.

"I seen 'em too," said Booger Tom. "I'd like to know who brung 'em."

"One minute!" bawled Ferris Blackmore.

All of the riders began to set for the start. Lourdes raised up once and then she set back down slowly, making sure her seat was perfect.

The crowd was dead silent.

The little popgun cracked and the horses sprang forward and

stayed on the line where they began. It was a straight race with no turns and so no advantage to moving in to a curve.

The race was over in three breaths and the camera on the tripod flashed and the horses and riders, now past the finish line, scattered and slowed.

Then one of the male jockeys stood up in his stirrups and he rode hard at Lourdes, his crop raised to slash at her.

Lourdes was looking away, but Stewball saw what was coming and he wheeled round and charged the other rider and horse and then he dodged away and was well out of reach.

A big heavy man in a western-cut suit began to run toward the horse and rider who had cut at Lourdes and Stewball.

The two men who had been at the camera ran at the horse and rider and one caught the bridle and then the rancher pounded up and he dragged the rider down and began to kick him as he lay on the ground till the others pulled him off.

The boy got up and the rancher kicked at him, and the boy ran away from the furious man, who was struggling to break free of the men who held him, and the boy climbed through the pasture fence and he ran on toward the county road.

The plane that had been droning lazily back and forth suddenly dropped down and flew directly overhead and the pilot waggled the wings and people quickly went to their rigs and pulled them forward while the riders brought the horses in.

Booger Tom held open the rear door for Stewball and Lourdes and the big horse got in before she took off the tack. Booger Tom and Du Pré shut the door and got in the truck and they drove toward the main gate, the first out of the place, and they turned right.

They went about four hundred yards and the rider who had run at Lourdes came up out of the barrow pit and he waved frantically.

Du Pré slowed down.

"You thinkin' what I am thinkin'?" said Booger Tom.

Du Pré nodded.

Booger Tom opened the door and leaned forward so the boy

could get in the jump seat in back. He dove in and Du Pré accelerated and the boy was so winded he was gasping for breath.

"*Gracias,*" he said.

"A Mex," said Booger Tom.

"One who has English," said the boy, "but thank you, señor, anyway."

His breathing had slowed.

Du Pré looked back in the rearview mirror when they got to the top of the first long hill. One pickup with trailer came out of the gate and turned away from them, and then Du Pré saw flashing lights beyond the truck.

"Road ahead is clear," said Booger Tom. "Must have come from Forsyth."

Du Pré nodded.

They drove on and the road was deserted, not a car or truck on it. They came half an hour later to a paved road and Du Pré turned north.

"A-mee-go," said Booger Tom, "you got no damn luck at all. You know who done pick you up? Girl you tried to whip is back in the trailer with the horse outfoxed you."

The boy lunged for the door, but Booger Tom grabbed his neck and he pressed with his thumb and the boy choked.

"Why'd you do a fool thing like that?" said Booger Tom.

"Mr. Travis says I win," the boy gasped, "he help me get my family here to America. I don't win, I go back, too. Mr. Travis he likes to win. So I am angry and foolish. Even when I run at her I was not going to do it. I am sorry."

"Good thing you didn't whip her," said Booger Tom. "She'd have kicked yer ass clear up around yer ears and then stomped you into the ground like a stake."

The boy quit gasping.

"What you going to do to me?" he said. "Mr. Travis, he find me he kill me. He killed other Mexicans I know."

"Who the hell is this Travis feller?" said Booger Tom.

"Ranchero," said the boy. "New Mexico, he has land, also Texas."

"What were you plannin' to do?" said Booger Tom. "Walk to Mexico?"

"Yes," said the boy. "It is better than coming home in a box."

"You look at me son," said Booger Tom. "You really wasn't going to hit the girl, Lourdes?"

The boy shook his head.

"I swear to it," he said.

"She may still kick your ass," said Booger Tom. "But I think we kin maybe help you."

The air got noisy. The little plane that had sounded the alarm flew over low, then rose up.

"Wonder if they saw us pick him up," said Booger Tom.

"They did not," said the boy. "I saw them fly the other way, or I would have stayed in the ditch."

CHAPTER

18

"I apologize," said the boy. "I am Tomás Guerrero and I apologize."

"So I beat you," said Lourdes, "you get your ass kicked by the rancher owns the horse that you are riding. Why are you so stupid?"

"Señor Travis tell me he will help me bring my family to America if I win," said Tomás.

"You trust that fat asshole?" said Lourdes.

The boy hung his head.

"Let's go eat," said Lourdes. She took his arm in her hand and pushed him toward the house.

Jacqueline looked at the pair of them.

"So," she said, "you win him, the race?"

"A long story," said Booger Tom.

"You two," said Jacqueline, "they are all long stories. Some of them are even true, but not very many. So now I got another kid, I think is the punch line this one."

"You were down a bit," said Booger Tom. "Inventory is back up, though."

"Very fun'," said Jacqueline. "Now what is this?"

"The kid charged Lourdes, the rancher owned the horse pulled him down, and he ran. We picked up the kid on the way out while the cops were coming in," said Booger Tom.

Du Pré was looking off to the mountains, well out of it.

"This little shit tries to run down my Lourdes?" said Jacqueline.

"He wasn't really," said Booger Tom. "I believe him. He wants to get his family out of Mexico. I expect his daddy's dead."

"That kid lucky he don't tangle with Lourdes," said Jacqueline. "She been kicking her brothers' asses all her life and most of theirs. You remember she got Alcide with the firewood that one time, laid him out cold?"

"No," said Booger Tom. "Not that it surprises me any."

"Him, he is pretty young to come up here, try send for his people," said Jacqueline.

Her heart opening like one big door, Du Pré thought.

"The feller he was ridin' for," said Booger Tom, "is not a very nice feller."

Du Pré looked at the old cowboy.

"You know him?" said Du Pré.

Booger Tom nodded.

"I never rode for him," he said, "but you hear things. Harry Travis has ranches in New Mexico and Texas, but the biggest one is in Mexico. Old family of pirates and thieves. Managed to hang on to it through the revolution and all. Had a friend went to ridin' for him, oh, thirty year ago, just flat disappeared. Went on to the New Mexico ranch, went with a load of stock to Mexico, never come back."

Du Pré looked at him.

"Travis's done about everything bad you kin think of," said Booger Tom. "Ol' Pinto was a nice feller but loose in the mouth department, so I expect he done spoke up when he should have shut up."

Du Pré nodded.

"That Mexican kid knows more than he's sayin'," said Booger Tom.

Du Pré nodded.

"I think," said Booger Tom, "it would be bad fer his health go back home to Mexico. What I think."

"That is fine," said Jacqueline, "but if they are coming here after him I should know that, yes?"

"Yup," said Booger Tom.

Du Pré rolled a smoke.

Jacqueline looked from one man to the other.

"We can't have him out to Bart's," said Booger Tom. "If he was seen, that would be the damned game."

"We maybe make it out with him they don't know," said Du Pré. "See what happens. He said the plane was going away and everybody else was all tangled up. We went quick because Stewball is so damn smart."

"Ok," said Jacqueline. "I think I maybe fix this. He is pret' fair-skinned kid."

Du Pré looked at her.

"Fix his hair," said Jacqueline. "Lots of Metis got that pale brown hair, you know."

Du Pré nodded.

"If they are looking for him hard," said Du Pré, "they maybe go to the Immigration people, put out posters."

"Then we would know anyway," said Jacqueline. "So they do that, we just send him up the cousins, Canada."

"OK," said Du Pré.

They got in the truck and drove out to Bart's with the empty horse trailer and they set it off on the block and parked the big double-tired pickup in the bay it lived in in the big steel shed.

They went in the house and Booger Tom made himself a tall glass of whiskey and soda.

Du Pré made one for himself.

"Ol' Pinto was a good feller," said Booger Tom. "I hadn't

thought about him till I heard that name. Travis. Harry Travis. Travis family had a couple patches in Cuba, too, I recall. Castro done took them and there was talk Harry's daddy was workin' with those fools tried to invade way back when. I ain't heard much since, but it wouldn't surprise me none he has been in on the trouble they had to Central America.

"I'se once about half drunk," said Booger Tom, "and I was in camp way the hell out the mountains south and west of here, damn near in the Park, and I come to the cook tent and go in and stumble a little, somebody's got their foot out. I cain't see cause the light out was so bright, and so I fire a boot in that direction and danged if it ain't a grizzly come in for a snack. I looked at him and he looked at me and I jumped straight back about a hundred feet, right through the door, and he come roaring out and another feller shot him."

Du Pré nodded.

"This," said Booger Tom, "looks to be a bit bigger than that lyin' sack of Blackfeet shit let on to us."

"Yah," said Du Pré.

"Blackmore is flat crazy," said Booger Tom, "but Harry Travis is a whole 'nother bear."

Booger Tom went out on the deck and he sat on a chair leaning forward with his drink in his hand. He looked off at the pasture on the far hill and the dots of black cattle on it.

"You got the good sense to be scairt?" said Booger Tom.

Du Pré nodded.

"It ain't about me," said Booger Tom, "but I wonder about takin' little Lourdes now, wonder about that, wonder about just what kind of bear we got in the tent now."

"Yah," said Du Pré.

The wind changed and got brisk from the west and a black line of clouds pooched up on the horizon. Soon they stretched clear across the western sky, the tops of them roiling.

"I think we will have one of them," said Booger Tom.

They went in and checked the windows and then Booger Tom went out to close up the barn.

There was a little pause and some dead air before the storm hit, but then it came and the wind pushed rain hard against the windows.

Tumbleweeds danced across the land.

Du Pré stood at the window, looking out at the blurred world.

CHAPTER

19

"These here Sand Hills are some kinda country," said Booger Tom, looking out at the Nebraska land.

"Crazy Horse is buried here," said Du Pré.

"Probably was better 'fore them rich peckerwoods found it," said Booger Tom. "Still looks pretty good, though."

Du Pré saw a big pullout off to the left. He waited for a stock hauler to pass, and he turned in and took the truck and trailer to the back. There was grass there and a few stubby pine trees. The view was of rolling round high hills.

They got out and unlocked the back door of the horse trailer and Stewball got out, and then Lourdes came a moment later leading one of the other Australian horses, Moondog. He was black with a white eye and white socks on his front feet.

Stewball ran a little, his tail held high, holding all his power and speed in. He snorted and shook his head.

Moondog looked longingly at Stewball.

Lourdes slipped off the halter and slapped Moondog on the rump and he looked at her unbelieving and then he ran after Stewball. The two horses raced down out of sight and were back in a moment.

"Got to go," said Booger Tom, looking at an old turnip watch he carried in his vest.

"Hey, you!" yelled Lourdes. "Get your ass over here."

Stewball nickered and danced away and the two of them ran on, and then Stewball turned and Moondog came behind and Stewball came in and he nuzzled Lourdes' hand while Moondog took off again.

"How 'bout," said Lourdes to the big horse, "you go and get that fool."

Stewball turned and ran off and was soon back with Moondog, shoving the gelding along with nips to the flanks. Moondog came to Lourdes to get away from Stewball, and Lourdes slipped the halter on and led the black into the trailer, and then she whistled and Stewball came in on his own.

"I wonder," said Booger Tom, "that big bastard fetches ducks."

"If Lourdes ask him to," said Du Pré.

They drove on, Booger Tom navigating, and then they turned onto a dirt road and went on down it for twenty miles. They came to a hidden small valley that held a ranch house and a couple of barns. The cottonwood trees that had once shielded the ranch house from the summer sun were all dead. Some had been cut down.

There were a dozen trucks and trailers there, and a few horses in small paddocks, each alone. There was no one out in the hot sun.

Two men came out of the ranch house when Du Pre pulled up. Booger Tom got out and he shook hands, laughing with the two men.

Du Pré looked.

I see them the other race, he thought, last one in Wyoming.

Blackmore is here, so that Anne-Marie is here, too.

Booger Tom came away from the two men and he motioned for Du Pre to follow him.

"Interestin'," he said. "They want to run the race at evening, not wait until tomorrow. Didn't say why."

Du Pré nodded.

"Anyhow," said Booger Tom, "we go on over by them dead trees there and let our ponies out to limber up. Two races, first one for colts, and Blackie Moondog there will go in that, and then the one for the money."

"Sell Moondog?" said Du Pré.

"If the money's right," said Booger Tom, "I might. Hard to say."

Du Pré nodded.

They got to the paddock and let the horses and Lourdes out.

There was a stock tank in one corner of the paddock, and Booger Tom pulled up the handle on the pump and water gushed into it.

Lourdes was out in the paddock, talking to the horses.

"Time was there was water here," said Booger Tom. "But Denver sucked everything out of the Platte and they pump too much out of the Oglalla pool down there. Lots of these places abandoned now, once had free flowin' springs, but not anymore, water table's down two hundred feet lower than it was, and sinking.

"Rode here a long time ago," said Booger Tom. "Next place over, actually. Sparked with the rancher's daughter, but she up and went off be a missionary someplace. I count it the narrowest escape of my life."

The old cowboy grinned.

Du Pré laughed.

"You shoulda seen the grass then they had here," said Booger Tom.

The hills were sparsely grown with clumps of tussock grasses, poor feed.

"West won't die of old age," said Booger Tom. "Be sucked dry."

They walked toward the ranch house and knocked at the door and heard laughter, loud male laughter.

There was a big sunny room at the back and twenty or so men, most of them Du Pré had seen at the other races.

"I go and see to Lourdes," whispered Du Pré. "I am just the hand."

He backed away, saw Booger Tom roaring at a couple of men.

Lourdes was carefully looking over Moondog's feet. Stewball was standing nearby, jealousy billowing off him.

Lourdes looked at the blue roan.

"I got to ride this one," she said. "We talked about it."

Stewball shook his head and looked disgusted. He went to the corner of the paddock to sulk.

"I maybe tape that right fetlock," said Du Pré. "Him, he throws his left in a little. I get the shoes right soon, but they are not yet."

"He will be good," said Lourdes. "But you better."

Du Pré went to the horse trailer and he got down the wrapping kit and he took out a roll of thin foam and some tape and he went back and wrapped Moondog's right fetlock carefully and he taped it off.

The black horse danced a little, not liking the bandage.

"He maybe don't need it," said Lourdes.

"But maybe he does," said Du Pré.

"Anne-Marie must be here," said Lourdes.

Du Pré nodded.

"She don't talk," said Lourdes. "I heard one of the men say he had never heard her say a word and Ferris Blackmore said she doesn't ever say anything unless it is real important."

Du Pré nodded.

"Something is wrong there I think," said Lourdes. "Anne-Marie, she tries to stare me down, the race, but then she always looks away first. I see sad in her eyes."

Du Pré nodded.

"So," said Lourdes. "We run Moondog first and Booger Tom maybe sells him. He is a good horse, but any other horse I talk to, Stewball tries to kill later . . . He is a funny horse."

"I put him the other paddock," said Du Pré.

"Talk to Moondog, Grandpapa," said Lourdes. "Stewball is in a pissy mood. He knows I am going to run Moondog and it makes him mad."

"OK," said Du Pré, laughing.

Three young cowboys in faded denims came out of the bunkhouse over near two tall dead cottonwoods. They each carried a shovel.

They went behind the trees and down and out of sight.

Du Pré petted Moondog's nose.

The horse fuffled, catching the scent of other horses in the breeze.

A small plane took off out of sight, engine snarling as it clawed into the air.

Sunlight flashed on the little silver plane.

Near time then, near time, Du Pré thought.

CHAPTER

20

"We got an hour," said Booger Tom.

"I don't see that Harry Travis," said Du Pré.

"He called," said Booger Tom. "Feller announced good old Harry would be here directly. I expect that is him now." He pointed at a light flashing on chrome at the top of the hill.

There were two gaudy double-tired pickups pulling matching trailers.

Du Pré left Booger Tom and Lourdes going over Moondog's feet and he walked over to the racetrack which began beyond the stand of dead cottonwoods. There was a long meadow there, gone to dry grass, and the three cowboys with the shovels were smoothing down the few tussocks remaining.

Be a damn desert soon enough . . . All of this . . . I come to the Sand Hills with Catfoot a couple of times, we go because Mama is mad at at him . . . long time gone.

Du Pré shook his head.

Another twelve-bay post had been set up, and there was a camera on a tripod at the finish line a quarter mile away.

Lots of money for a quarter mile, quarter horses are the drag racers of horses, very fast for that time . . . cow horses, got to move but not so far.

Music came from the ranch house, Bob Wills and the Texas Playboys.

Good music, that.

Du Pré looked at the post and he found nothing much wrong with it. The races were honest because the people weren't.

But what does poor Badger have to do with this? They will not take to some new feller don't have friends.

How long till somebody recognizes Booger Tom or me?

I am just a breed, though.

Du Pré walked back to the paddock. Men were coming out of the ranch house now and going to their horses, the riders dressed in tight clothes.

Anne-Marie Schroeder was walking with Ferris Blackmore. She wore a black helmet, the kind steeplechase riders wore.

They stopped at a paddock that had a different horse in it.

Du Pré stared at the horse for a moment.

Big bay, pretty young gelding, spirited.

The horse backed away from Anne-Marie. She had to keep talking softly to him and get slowly up to him to slip on the halter and even then he still shied a few times when she started to put on the saddle and bridle.

Lourdes beat her twice, twice she come in second and that other time third, when Tomás beat her, but Lourdes still won.

Harvey, he was very eager to talk, Tomás.

Du Pré laughed.

Kid was really stubborn, wouldn't come to Harvey, Harvey couldn't come to Montana.

Spend a lot of time on the telephone, those two.

Tomás, him, he blend in with Jacqueline's brood ver' god-damned quick.

Du Pré laughed.

He went back to the truck and he took his flask from under the seat and he had some bourbon and he smoked.

Booger Tom and Lourdes had Moondog saddled and bridled.

Stewball hung his head over the fence and he looked so mourn-ful that Du Pré laughed every time he looked at him.

Lourdes left Moondog and she went to poor Stewball and pet-ted his nose and talked to him for a while. Then there was a lot of motion, riders leading the horses toward the post and Lourdes and Booger Tom went, too.

The cell phone in the glove box chirred, and Du Pré fished it out.

"You there?" said Harvey.

"Yah," said Du Pré.

"What's happening?"

"First race a few minutes," said Du Pré.

"Those guys you saw in Wyoming, the ones who were also at the place in Montana, dressed in black, you get a good look at them?"

"Some," said Du Pré.

"You have a camera?" said Harvey.

"Yah," said Du Pré.

"Get a picture if you can," said Harvey. "Wouldn't do to stay on this long, no telling what they have there." And he hung up.

Du Pré sighed and he took the small digital camera out of its case and he tried to remember how it worked.

Easy. Point it and press that.

No flash.

Du Pré put it in his shirt pocket. He yawned.

Race time, three, five minutes.

He felt sleepy.

There was a movement in the side mirror and Du Pré looked and he saw one of the men Harvey wanted a picture of walking carefully up toward the cab.

Du Pré opened the door and he got out.

"Afternoon," he said.

One of the other men appeared on the far side of the truck and Du Pré could see the third on the porch of the ranch house.

All coming to see what is in the truck.

"You want something?" said Du Pré.

The man looked at him levelly.

"No," said the man. "We were just on our way to the race. Dave Wilson has a horse in it again."

"Yah," said Du Pré.

"He has very good horses," said the man.

The accent was strange, not one Du Pré knew.

Him don't speak English first.

"Yah," said Du Pré.

He walked away from them, and they met the man who had been at the house and they followed along.

Du Pré looked back once, they all had on identical dark glasses and they all were grim-faced.

Lourdes was already in position when Du Pré got there, and he came up behind Booger Tom, who was laughing with Harry Travis.

Travis's big red face was split in a warm grin, but his gray eyes were cold in the flesh.

"Ol' Moon Dawg'll fly," said Booger Tom.

The bets were being taken. Right up to the post.

Booger Tom had already laid his money down.

Du Pré waited patiently for Booger Tom to not notice him.

When the old cowboy looked at him, Du Pré flicked his eyes once at the three men in the black clothes so out of place in Nebraska's summer heat.

Booger Tom seemed not to see, but then he stuck his left hand to his ear, so he had.

Du Pré slipped the camera out of his pocket.

"Two to post!" yelled Ferris Blackmore.

When the race began everyone was interested, and Du Pré got three shots of the men in the black clothes, profiles, but better than nothing.

He put the camera back in his pocket.

Moondog came in second, and Anne-Marie and her big bay came in first.

The two girls ran their horses for a long ways out, while the other riders returned.

They went up and over the first hill.

"God damn that kid!" yelled Harry Travis.

CHAPTER
21

Harry Travis raged for a time, and then he shut up and stalked off fuming, and the three men Du Pré had photographed went after him and so did a few others. Booger Tom sauntered on. He had his hands in his pockets and he was whistling.

Lourdes and Anne-Marie appeared soon enough, coming in to the starting bays, dismounting, and then both girls began to walk their horses to cool them.

Stewball let fly an indignant whinny and Lourdes looked at Du Pré.

"You take Moondog," she said. "I got to go and soothe Stewball."

Du Pré took the reins, slipped off the headstall and put on a halter. He led Moondog to the trailer, stripped off the saddle, stuck it on the hood of the truck along with the reins and headstall and the little blanket pad and then he led Moondog away from Stewball, who was glaring at the black horse murderously.

"I hope we sell you," said Du Pré to Moondog. "You will not make it home alive the same trailer, Stewball."

Moondog was sweating and Du Pré moved a little faster. The black horse was in fine shape and soon his breathing slowed and the wind dried his coat and Moondog tossed his head.

"You want some water," said Du Pré. He led the black horse to the stock tank and let him drink a little, pulling him away before he had had as much as he wanted. Du Pré walked him for another fifteen minutes and let him drink again.

Then he put him in the paddock. Lourdes had already taken Stewball out of his paddock and saddled him and put on the head-stall and she was walking slowly to the starting bays, stopping every few feet to talk softly to the blue roan, who was still furious.

Du Pré went back to the pickup and he took the saddle from the hood and he put it in the tack bay on its rack and he went round to the other side and to the passenger door and he bent over and looked at the seam where the door fit on the body.

Du Pré nodded.

So somebody is in here looking for something, don't find much.

The camera was still in his pocket.

Du Pré checked the pistol in the side pocket in the door. He pulled the slide back.

There was a round in the chamber and there had not been.

He checked the glove box. It looked cluttered.

There was no one around. Du Pré went to the tack bay and he opened it and he reached up overhead and found the Schmeisser, which was hidden behind a padded crosspiece that was not visible from the door.

Du Pré got the two pistols and the other had a round in the chamber, too. He emptied all of the 9mm rounds both held, put them in a trash bin, and replaced them with fresh ammunition, and then he put them back in the door pockets, one on each side.

There was a burst of loud voices coming from the ranch house, and the front door opened and the men who had gone in with Harry Travis and Ferris Blackmore came out.

A few were laughing and the others looked grim.

The riders and horses were gathering for the second race.

Booger Tom was talking with a man who wore Las Vegas cowboy clothes, garish in cut and color, and they shook hands.

There goes Moondog, Du Pré thought.

Lourdes had found a patch of shade near a shed, and she was standing there talking to Stewball, who was looking a little more cheerful.

Booger Tom and the Las Vegas cowboy were laughing a little too hard at each other's jokes.

Du Pré waited by the truck. Booger Tom and the Las Vegas cowboy came over.

"This here's Benny Fletcher," said Booger Tom. "He done bought that Moon Dawg and so I suppose we oughta give him the papers."

Du Pré nodded, fished them out of the glove box, and he handed them to Booger Tom.

"I'd pay a lot for that other one," said Benny.

"Ain't fer sale," said Booger Tom. "I like winnin'."

"So," said Benny Fletcher, "do I. Moon Dawg can run good now. I work him some, maybe we'll beat you. Damn horse ain't been worked enough."

Like we thought to do, Du Pré thought.

Booger Tom and Benny Fletcher shook hands and Fletcher walked away.

Booger Tom took a very thick bundle of hundred-dollar bills from his coat pocket.

"Down payment," he said. "Got a check fer the rest, and I do expect that it is good."

Du Pré nodded.

"Lourdes is gonna take this race," said Booger Tom. "And she coulda on Moon Dawg, she hadn't started him wrong, which of course she did a-purpose. It's the next race worries me."

Du Pré bent close and Booger Tom whispered. "I just joined up with the patriots," he said. "Give them ten grand to fight the Com-

mies, niggers, and Jews. On account of they got so many workin'
for them, they are a little soft on Mexicans and half-breeds, so I
guess we kin keep on."

"Somebody is through the truck looking," whispered Du Pré.

"We got a foot in the door," said Booger Tom. "But I can't help
thinkin' about that goddamned grizzly in the tent."

Du Pré nodded.

"Five to post!" yelled Ferris Blackmore.

The riders and horses milled near the green gates set into bays.

"Wal," said Booger Tom, "let's us go and win some money."

The riders set their horses, Ferris Blackmore fired his little popgun and Stewball shot out of the bay and stayed a full length ahead
for the full race and was pulling farther ahead when the horses
crossed the finish line.

Lourdes stood in her stirrups to slow Stewball down, but the
blue roan was ready to run and he flew up the hill and along the
crest and then he thundered down it and only then would he con-
sent to be slowed.

The watcher in the plane was still circling, so there was no one
coming.

Lourdes brought Stewball to the trailer and she got down and
stripped off the saddle and blanket and headstall, and she put a
halter on him and she led him round and round in a tight circle.

Booger Tom was talking and laughing with Ferris Blackmore
and Travis and Fletcher. Then Booger Tom went to the bet table
and got a shoebox full of money and he came back to the trailer.

"I tol' them we had to make tracks," said Booger Tom, "but I
would visit ol' Ferris in a few days."

Lourdes put Stewball in the trailer and she shut the back gate
and she got in the jump seat of the pickup. Du Pré and Booger
Tom got in and Du Pré started the engine and they pulled away
and went down the ranch road, over the dry and dying Sand Hills,
bled out by Denver.

Booger Tom looked at the country.

"That's about what is happenin' to the West I once knew," he said, and he shook his head.

"How are you not riding with Stewball?" said Du Pré.

Lourdes leaned over the seat.

"Anne-Marie said that I shouldn't come to the next race," said Lourdes. "She said it would be very dangerous. She didn't know why exactly, but she said she was scared herself."

CHAPTER

22

Du Pré heard the plane coming in and there was a high shriek as the engines on the small jet were reversed and then the plane appeared, slowing rapidly.

The little jet wheeled round to the private hangars and Du Pré walked out toward it. A door opened and folded down to become a stairway.

Madelaine came down the steps and she flung her arms around Du Pré and they kissed for a long time. The pilot brought down some luggage. He set the suitcases around Du Pré and Madelaine and he got back in the little jet and the stairway folded up and the plane began to move back toward the runway.

They were still kissing when the little jet screamed down the concrete and rose into the air.

They came up for air.

"I miss you," said Du Pré.

"I think so," said Madelaine. "Me, I miss you."

They carried Madelaine's luggage out to the old cruiser and they put it in the trunk and got in and drove to the first motel and Du Pré rented a room and they fucked for a good long time.

After, Du Pré rolled a smoke and he put it to Madelaine's lips and he flicked his lighter and she drew in the smoke and handed the cigarette to Du Pré.

"OK," said Madelaine. "Important stuff is done for now. Anybody die I am gone?"

"*Non,*" said Du Pré.

"So you come back with another kid, this Tomás?" said Madelaine.

"Yah," said Du Pré. "He is riding one of the ranchers, goes after Lourdes, whip up, Stewball sees, runs, then the guy he works for knocks him around and the kid runs, and he has the thumb out we go by, we are first gone from there. So I bring him back, Toussaint, and Jacqueline folds him in, her bunch. Harvey is ver' excited, this kid tells him about things on Harry Travis's ranch, Mexico."

Madelaine nodded.

"But me," said Du Pré, "I think he is not what he says he is."

Madelaine nodded.

"So before I go, I say, Alcide, who Tomás is closest to, Alcide, I ask you maybe see you find anything Tomás has hid," said Du Pré.

Madelaine looked at him.

"Everything is fine we go here and there," said Du Pré. "Then, last time, somebody goes through the pickup, not so thorough, they do not have time, but they do it, are careful we don't see them."

"OK," said Madelaine. "But what is this Tomás doing?"

"He maybe has a cell phone," said Du Pré. "He ruins his clothes he is riding in, but he has been to Billings twice, we give him three hundred, buy clothes so Alcide can have his back, so Tomás buys clothes, maybe he buys something else."

"You got this mind like a raven's," said Madelaine. "So why you think all this?"

"Because," said Du Pré, "I think this Travis, who is ver' powerful, if him want Tomás back there be something, Immigration, maybe police. But there is nothing. Tomás say that Travis will help get his family here to America he wins these horse races. I maybe don't think so. I think maybe Tomás family is in this, maybe hostages, Travis's Mexican ranch or something."

"OK," said Madelaine. "So when we get back, maybe Alcide knows something."

"Or maybe Tomás is what him say," said Du Pré. "But it all fits together too good. He is right where we pass, they know we will leave first because that Stewball is so easy, load, and the plane comes over us after we go, I wonder out loud, Tomás says no, the plane it is going the other way when he gets out of the ditch."

"Not enough time the plane to turn," said Madelaine.

"Him say nothing," said Du Pré. "I feel better than I do when he did."

"So," said Madelaine. "Maybe they know that you and Booger Tom are not who you say you are."

"I think maybe," said Du Pré. "They got no reason go through the truck unless they got a reason, but what is the reason?"

"So," said Madelaine. "But it is not Tomás so much, since they send him, they already know."

"Yah," said Du Pré.

"This," said Madelaine, "is not so good."

"No," said Du Pré. "It is not."

"So," said Madelaine. "You want to screw some more now and then we maybe stop that store you like, get some road food, go home?"

An hour later they left the delicatessen with some soppressata and asiago cheese and some olives and beer. A couple of baguettes.

Du Pré drove only ten miles over the speed limit on the Interstate, but when he turned north he floored it, and the cruiser shot down the road, empty ahead, though Du Pré slowed way down when he went over a hill in case there was a tractor with a trailer full of hay going seven miles an hour on the other side out of sight.

But most of the road was clear to view.

They ate and drank beer. Du Pré rolled a smoke one-handed while the car did a hundred and ten and he handed it to Madelaine who lit it and took the one drag she liked.

"How is that Pallas?" said Du Pré.

"Ha," said Madelaine. "She is somebody else's problem now, yes, and it will be restful, me and Jacqueline. She is in this place got sort of houseparents and doctors ask stupid questions half the time and she is about half pissed Ripper is off doing something she can't hunt him down the streets of Washington."

Du Pré laughed.

"She is doing this math for them. She likes that, plays with her computer all the time. I did not know she liked music so much. She plays the piano there, there are four of them, the house. You never play the piano, do you?"

"Non," said Du Pré.

"I try," said Madelaine. "It don't work."

"She got music anyway," said Du Pré.

"That Raymond," said Madelaine, "his Scotch blood is the piano."

Du Pré laughed. Raymond's mother's name had been MacDougal. After 1763, the English took over the fur trade and the Scots came to run it.

"Him Fortier," said Du Pré. "I don't think there is that much Scotch blood, him."

"We get home," said Madelaine, "I hear you play your fiddle, yes?"

Du Pré nodded. He had slowed down to forty going over a hill, and a good thing, for just beyond it the whole road was full of Hereford cattle. They slowed way down and edged through the herd. A cowboy on an Appaloosa touched his hat and after they passed through the last of the herd and were well away Du Pré gunned the engine and they got up to cruising speed again.

The Wolf Mountains began to rise up in the north and the land began to shelf up to them, an island range thrust up through the earth.

Du Pré got to the crossroads at the west end of the mountains and he turned right and then he shot toward Toussaint.

They went to Madelaine's house and in.

There was one message on the machine.

"Papa, you get back, you come right away," said Jacqueline.

Du Pré carried in the suitcases and set them down.

"I am going, too," said Madelaine.

They went to Raymond and Jacqueline's.

Alcide and Jacqueline and Tomás were in the kitchen.

Tomás had a shiner and a split lip.

There was a small black cell phone on the kitchen table.

CHAPTER

23

"Let me read it back once," said Foote. He spoke the cell phone numbers.

"That is it," said Du Pré.

"Give me a minute," said Foote, and he switched off.

Du Pré held the telephone to his shoulder and he looked at Tomás, who had laid his head down on the table and was crying silently.

"OK," said Foote.

"I don't call Harvey," said du Pré. "I don't think I better."

"No," said Foote. "For what it is worth he would just have sent it to me anyway."

"Yah," said Du Pré.

"I'll call back, I guess," said Foote. "Not that I think it means much if he didn't."

Du Pré hung up. He went to the kitchen table and he tapped Tomás on the shoulder. The boy raised his head.

"In a few minutes," said Du Pré, "I will know if you were lying. You say you make not calls, that telephone."

Tomás shook his head.

Du Pré sat down.

"Tell me again what Harry Travis tell you," said Du Pré.

"He tell me to fake attacking Lourdes," said Tomás, "and he say I should get picked up by you, tell you he would kill me, then find out who you were."

Du Pré nodded.

"You do that pret' good," said Du Pré.

"Stewball is some horse," said Tomás. "He just gets in the trailer. So you will always be the first to leave."

"And so you go and buy this, Billings," said Du Pré, pointing at the cell phone.

Tomás nodded.

"But you say you never use it," said Du Pré.

"I don't," said Tomás. "You are too good to me."

"Your family?" said Du Pré.

"My father is dead, I told you that," said Tomás. "My mother and four sisters are on Señor Travis's estancia in Torreón. They want to come to America. There is so little in Mexico, except for the rich."

"You think Travis will hurt your people?" said Du Pré.

"I tell you he kills," said Tomás. "There are many buried on the rancho. Everyone knows that."

Du Pré nodded.

"Why does he want to know who we are?" said Du Pré.

Tomás shook his head.

"He does not say," said Tomás, "but his foreman on the rancho, New Mexico, says these people who race the horses are always trying, put one over on each other. Bring in a horse that runs well no one knows about. They have much money and enjoy cheating each other."

The telephone rang. Du Pré went to it.

"No use at all," said Foote.

Du Pré went round the corner.

"This is maybe not so bad," said Du Pré. "Bart tell me once that he, back when he is drinking, he loses a lot of money gambling."

"Oh, yes," said Foote. "Our office settled many of those debts."

"So maybe Bart is getting back to gambling," said Du Pré.

Foote was silent for a time.

"If that is all that this is," he said.

"I think maybe it is," said Du Pré. "Nothing goes on, these races, but big betting. There were three men there I took pictures of, Alcide sent them to Harvey over the computer, I do not know how."

"Harvey know who they are?" said Foote.

"He has not called," said Du Pré. "They went to his home, not to his office."

"So," said Foote. "If that worked, and it could—"

"This big race in three weeks," said Du Pré. "There is something there I think. Not the race, something else."

"You want to do it," said Foote.

"Yes," said Du Pré. "I think so."

"We might learn a lot in three weeks," said Foote.

"Yah," said Du Pré.

He put the telephone up.

Tomás was not at the table. There was water running in the bathroom.

The boy came out, toweling his face.

"What you think Travis will do, your people?" said Du Pré.

Tomás shook his head.

"I don't know," he said. "He say I can have them come to New Mexico and work on his rancho, he will help them get papers."

"There are three men there, wearing city clothes, boots that lace," said Du Pré. "You know them, they all wear black, all wear sunglasses?"

Tomás shook his head.

"I don't know," he said. "When we run in Texas there are very

113

many people there, most of them city people. But I don't remember three men in black clothes."

"OK," said Du Pré. "Here is what we do. You stay here, keep quiet. We will do this big race, then see about your people. But you got to stay here."

"Yes," said Tomás, "I do that."

"OK," said Du Pré. "You tell me the truth about the phone, you do this, I help you with your family. What did your father die of?"

"Truck accident," said Tomás. "He was a driver, he gets an old truck, brakes don't work, he goes off this mountain road."

Du Pré nodded.

Madelaine had been leaning against a wall in the kitchen.

She yawned.

"OK," she said. "Me, I want to go to bed, sleep some."

She grabbed Du Pré and they went out to the cruiser and he drove to her place. She went to the kitchen and made tea and she looked through the mail.

"Thierry is doing well, has leave in two months, wants to come here and see me," she said.

Du Pré nodded. Her oldest son was a master sergeant in the marines, stationed in Korea.

Younger boy was in the marines in Germany.

"Robert is still playing the fiddle and Susie is expecting," said Madelaine.

She tossed all of the advertising in the trash.

"Pallas is not here hiding out," said Madelaine. "It is so quiet."

Du Pré laughed.

"So you go with Booger Tom to see this Blackmore?" said Madelaine.

Du Pré nodded.

"Leave in the morning," he said.

Madelaine yawned.

She went off to the bedroom and she undressed and got under the covers. Du Pré stood in the doorway.

"You sleep," said Du Pré. "Me, I have to talk to that Harvey."

CHAPTER
24

Du Pré went under the log arch at the ranch gate. There were five royal elk racks on the front of the crosspiece, and the skull of a bighorn sheep, with full curl horns.

A mile down the road they came to a triple fork, one that had a sign on the right one that said MAIN RANCH and an arrow made of rusted steel pipe.

"I never made enough money to bother over taxes," said Booger Tom. "I got to remember how communistic I think they are. Actually, I think they are."

"You will do fine," said Du Pré, laughing.

"I expect," said Booger Tom, "if this crazy son of a bitch really does have a shrine to Hitler I will gag some. I was with the first troops went into Theresienstadt concentration camp. After that, we done killed any SS we found."

Du Pré drew in on his smoke.

"I expect you are supposed to stay with the truck or some shit," said Booger Tom, "which just means you are lucky."

"Yah," said Du Pré.

"I was you," said Booger Tom, "I would not poke around any."

Du Pré snorted.

They came round the side of the mountain and saw the main ranch buildings down below, in a lovely pocket meadow above the benchlands that stretched off to the east. There was a big white house, the old-style high-gabled Victorian clapboard building, and then some metal barns and sheds and a weathered gray horse barn that looked old enough.

Du Pré pulled up by the main house and he parked.

"Tonier place than the other one," said Booger Tom. "Tucked up in the hills here. Quite a view."

Ferris Blackmore appeared in the front door and he came across the wide covered porch and down the steps, smiling.

Booger Tom got out and he limped over to Blackmore and they shook hands and walked on inside.

Du Pré shook his head. He rolled down the window of the pickup and he yawned.

Madelaine come back she damn near kill me.

Du Pré fished the plastic flask out from under the seat and he had some bourbon and he rolled a smoke.

The front door of the main house opened, and Anne-Marie Schroeder came out carrying a tray that had lemonade and a plate of sandwiches on it. She brought the tray to the truck and she came round to Du Pré.

"Here," she said. "I thought you might be hungry."

She does speak, maybe just not at races.

"Thank you very much," said Du Pré.

"You're welcome," said Annie-Marie. She went back up the steps and into the house.

Du Pré lifted the sandwich.

Cheese and salami.

He was hungry and he ate. The lemonade was fresh.

When he was finished he lifted the plate to put the paper napkin under it, and he saw a slip of paper.

Du Pré picked it up. It was folded in half and had Lourdes' name on the front. Du Pré tucked it into his shirt pocket and he snapped the flap.

Du Pré sat for two hours, and then a cowboy came to the truck and said if he wanted supper he could eat with the hands in the cookhouse over by the three trailers where the cowboys bunked.

Du Pré nodded.

"Half an hour," said the cowboy.

Du Pré wandered over to the cookhouse twenty minutes later and he found nine men there, chaffing each other, and a stout elderly woman brought out big platters of fried chicken and bread, mashed potatoes and gravy, biscuits, and triple-bean salad. The food was very good and the young men ate hugely.

Du Pré finished and he carried his plate to the kitchen and saw several pies there, so he waited for them and one was huckleberry and he had two pieces and some bunkhouse coffee.

The coffee would float a horseshoe.

He went to the kitchen to thank the cook, and she just nodded, and she started to wash the huge piles of dishes.

"I would help you," said Du Pré.

She smiled then and Du Pré dried dishes for a while and then he took over the scrubbing and soon enough they were all done and the pots and pans and pie dishes were set to soak a bit. They both had a smoke at the table in the kitchen.

"Name's Dora," said the woman. She reached down under the table for a bottle and she had a long pull at it and she offered it to Du Pré and he had one, too.

Cook ain't drunk the food's no good, and never, ever mess with the cook.

"Been here long?" said Du Pré.

"Eight years," said Dora. "I used to have a restaurant and a husband but they both up and went. My ma was a cook and I am, too. There are lots worse lives. I have lived a couple of them." She laughed, showing her missing teeth.

"I come about horses," said Du Pré.

"I allus liked horses better'n people," said Dora.

"I have some bourbon in the truck," said Du Pré. "I will get it." And he went to the pickup and got a half gallon from the box in the back and he went back to the cookhouse.

Dora looked greedily at the big bottle.

Du Pré got a couple of glasses down from a cupboard and he poured generous measures into each.

"Such good food," he said, "I give you the whiskey. I have more."

"I thank you," said Dora. "I git to town often but whiskey is a costly thing."

They drank.

Dora had been all over the ranch. From time to time she took a horse and rode, on her days off.

It was a big place with four thousand head of cattle on it and two hundred horses.

Mister Blackmore was an OK boss, though he had a bad temper.

The hands stayed about as long as hands did, the only two who were there this year who had been there last year were the mechanics who worked on the machinery.

"He has wheat," said Du Pré.

"Naw," said Dora. "Just cattle. Does a section of hay, irrigated."

Du Pré nodded.

Dora leaned forward.

"He's got a big room built underground," she said, drunk, wanting to share confidences."

Du Pré nodded.

"Got two airplanes in it," said Dora. "There's a runway there in the grass."

"He has two other airplanes in a hangar there," said Dora. "And a windsock and some other radio stuff, but you can't see the underground hangar. The door lifts up, it has grass and shrubs on it."

"Ever been in it?" said Du Pré.

Dora shook her head.

"All locked up," she said. "But I saw it open once, Blackmore didn't know I was there."

CHAPTER

25

Du Pré heard the sound of truck engines and he left Dora crooning to the last pot as she scrubbed it halfheartedly.

New pickups, usually with double rear axles, and expensive SUVs came in twos and threes and they parked here and there near the old white ranch house, and men and a few women got out and wandered up to the place. The long summer light had another hour.

Some of the people had drivers and they lit smokes and lounged around whatever it was they had driven, not looking at each other.

A small plane flew over low and set down beyond a stand of cottonwoods and the snarling engine cut back and not thirty seconds later another, a twin-engine this time, set down, and a few minutes later a third.

A cowboy in a big SUV drove past, and he was soon back with a load of people from the airplanes.

A few more vehicles came in.

Sixty people, Du Pré figured.

Booger Tom wandered out of the ranch house and he came to Du Pré with a tall can of beer, unopened.

"Wal," he said. "Thought you'd be thirsty. I was about right. He ain't got a shrine to good ol' Adolf but he is flat convinced little ol' George Bush is a Communist and he durn near fell over from apoplexy at the name of Clinton. He bitched for a time about that Communist Franklin Roosevelt rottin' America about to death and he had his way Ronald Reagan woulda lived forever, and like that there. I got little use fer the federal government, but they is so incompetent at anything they do it don't matter all that much, and the folks come is of a like mind. They are convinced the liberals mean to steal their property and it is time to fight back."

Du Pré nodded.

"So," said Booger Tom, "about all I know is when I bet I put down good money, and when I win I get money and a check. Last time all I got was the check. Perfectly good check. I guess what I oughta find out is what home the money finds. All them hundred dollar bills."

Du Pré nodded.

Booger Tom got several bundles of hundreds from the small safe welded to the truck frame under the step bumper in the back of the truck.

"This strikes me," he said, "as the sort of meeting where the hat gets passed and I think I oughta contribute. I wondered how ol' Ferris was on the Eye-talian question, but he done told me he admired Mussolini so I guess Bart won't mind I give off fifty grand to such a fair-minded feller."

Du Pré laughed.

Booger Tom took a quick look at the other drivers.

"Blond and blue-eyed to a man," he said. "You watch your ass while I am in there. I ain't brought up the Injun question but I expect the answer would be kinda abrupt."

The old cowboy went back in.

A record of the national anthem began to play, and after it was over there were cheers and whistles.

Du Pré got back in the cab of the truck and he lit a smoke.

Two county sheriff's cruisers came down the road and four deputies got out and they went in the house.

Du Pré nodded.

He sat there for two hours, and from time to time there were cheers and clappings loud enough to hear.

People began to leave then in twos and threes and Booger Tom was among the last. He came out talking fast to Ferris Blackmore, and they shook hands at the top of the steps and Booger Tom came down them and he walked to the truck Du Pré sat in.

Du Pré started the engine and the old cowboy got in and Du Pré wheeled round and he got behind a canary-yellow SUV with a big American flag decal on the rear window.

"That danged flag is about right," said Booger Tom. "Them fools in that piss-yeller shitwagon ain't got a clue what it means, and way they set it they'll never know what is comin' up behind them."

Du Pré laughed.

They went down the long ranch road to the country road and turned right while the SUV went left. Du Pré gunned the engine. There was a long line of headlights coming out and he saw the winking lights of a plane low and rising off to the west.

"That," said Booger Tom, "was so danged funny I had a rough time keepin' my face straight. I done it but it was danged hard."

Du Pré reached under the seat for the flask and he had a pull and he handed it to Booger Tom.

"Ferris Blackmore done made a speech," he said. "And then there was a feller dressed in cammies informed us that America had done gone communistic during the Lincoln administration. It was bad enough the niggers got freed, but the real trouble come from going off the gold standard. He thought if the only money was gold, things would be much better. Then there was a feller sellin' bunks in a fallout shelter he done built on his ranch. Then there was another feller talked about patriotism and the Patriots and then the hat got passed, and, I tell you, that was one fat hat time it come back to him. Had to send it out four times. I got no idea how many dollars four big hatsful is, but that is what he got and they was handin' him more later."

"I think Blackmore has one of those planes," said Du Pré. "The cook said there was an underground hangar over by the airstrip."

"I allus thought that was just a rumor," said Booger Tom.

"No," said Du Pré. "They've been looking for them for forty years."

"It don't surprise me," said Booger Tom. "You know that little gal rides for Ferris? Her ma was in there, too, good-lookin' blond lady. She was ravin' about the abortionists."

Du Pré nodded.

"I worked for a few ranchers shoulda been in a rubber room," said Booger Tom. "There was one of them there tonight but he didn't know me. He didn't know me when I worked for him, neither."

Du Pré laughed.

"I was invisible," said Du Pré. "So were the others, though the cowboys saw I got dinner."

"So did I," said Booger Tom. "Fer yer information, the rich eat pretty bad. Anne-Marie's mother cooked it. It was said to be real healthy for ya."

Du Pré snorted and he rolled a smoke and gave his pouch and papers to Booger Tom.

"There's goin' to be some wingding at that Dakota race," said Booger Tom. "Said there would be a big surprise for folks."

Du Pré nodded.

"They could see where their money was a-goin'," said Booger Tom.

A mule deer buck jumped through the lamp beams, his antlers in velvet.

Du Pré slowed down.

Four more deer crossed the road.

A pair of headlights crested a hill five miles behind them.

Du Pré speeded up again.

"See some that next crick," said Booger Tom. "After that they will have bedded down for the night. They's movin' now."

They drove on west in the soft dark.

CHAPTER

26

"Irish Republican Army," said Harvey over the telephone. "Two of them were on the British Most Wanted list. Bomb makers. The other guy just handles money. Very bad people."

"What are they doing horse racing in Nebraska?" said Du Pré.

"What are they doing on earth?" said Harvey. "See, all the gangs and all the dingdongs are hooking up. The Internet. The IRA was once a political terror group, now they are just dope runners and thugs. Then there is money. Money now lives on wires. It flits around the world. Now that Europe has a single currency, it is very easy to hide it, move it, send it about anywhere, and the cops are always well behind. It is a really great time to be a criminal or a terrorist."

"OK," said Du Pré. "But this is all going someplace, and I, me, I would like to know where, so when I get shot I will know why."

"It used to be," said Harvey, "that these assholes had less mobility and a lot more trouble moving money and themselves. But along with everything else in these parlous modern times, it got a lot faster. And fast is very dangerous for the rest of us. Those idiots you took Booger Tom to join the other night are so stupid they probably need metronomes just to breathe, but they are useful. They bankroll a lot of things they would be very upset about if they knew. They never will."

"So," said Du Pré, "I am told there will be some big surprise at this race, South Dakota."

"So I understand," said Harvey. "Don't worry, we have Ripper there, him and his godawful teeth, and we are interested enough so there will be other eyeballs on the party."

"OK," said Du Pré.

"You still got that machine pistol?" said Harvey.

"*Non,*" said Du Pré. "You know I never had one."

"I'll send you some really good oil," said Harvey. "Makes the slide run even faster. Bye, now."

Du Pré hung up the telephone.

Madelaine was at the bar talking with Susan Klein while Benny, the county sheriff, ate a cheeseburger and a mound of fries.

Bart came in, his overalls freshly cleaned. His red face was chapped and cracked from wind and sun.

Madelaine got up and she went to him and kissed his cheek.

Bart smiled, but his eyes looked sad for a moment, and then he brightened.

He sat next to Madelaine and Du Pré sat next to him, and Bart got up to move so Du Pré could be with his woman.

"Sit," said Madelaine. "I heard all his jokes."

"OK," said Bart. "But I don't have any new ones."

Madelaine looked at him.

"You call her?" she said.

Bart flushed beet red.

"No," he said.

"OK," said Madelaine. "What are we going to do, you, so you call her."

"She is the most beautiful woman I ever saw," said Bart. "What would she want to have anything to do with me for?"

Madelaine looked at Susan, at Benny, at Du Pré.

"It is a ver' good question," said Madelaine, "why good women like me, Susan, others, have anything to do at all with you morons. Very good question. Susan, you got an answer to that question maybe?"

"No," said Susan, "I lose sleep over it."

"Fer chrissake," said Benny.

"OK," said Madelaine. "Me, Bart are going to go call her."

"I need a drink," Bart whined. "I can't do this."

"Give this shithead a ginger ale," said Madelaine. "Double lime, make it real strong."

Susan mixed the drink and she set it in front of Bart.

"We go to my house," said Madelaine. "That way there are not so many people make you nervous."

"You're enough," said Bart, standing up.

"Yah," said Madelaine. "I mean to be."

They went out. A car engine started.

"Would somebody tell me what this is about?" said Benny, looking very puzzled.

Susan grinned evilly.

"Bart is about as dumb as most of you turkeys," said Susan, "and there is this spectacular woman who is crazy about him, and Bart, who can't see it at all, won't believe it even when he gets told. He is about to take that dragline he loves so much, dig a deep hole, and hide in it. So when Madelaine is back getting Pallas into a cage in Baltimore, this lady and Madelaine have a nice dinner and they get shitfaced and it comes out that she is mad for Bart, who doesn't seem to know she is alive. So Madelaine promises to take him by the ear and make him call her."

Benny nodded and bit a last french fry.

"OK," said Benny.

Du Pré snorted.

Benny looked at him.

"Who is it?" said Benny. "Some East Coast lady I don't know?"

"You know her," said Susan. "You lost a patrol car over her. Remember when Lufkin ran into the parked ice-cream truck that time?"

"Yeah," said Benny. "He said the power steering went out."

"That," said Susan Klein, "is indeed what he said."

"He lied to me?" said Benny.

"Lufkin is married to Anna," said Susan. "Very tough lady, Anna, so yes, indeedy-do, he lied like a dawg."

"It wasn't the power steering?" said Benny.

"Nope," said Susan. "It was not. It was this lady who is so very, very good-lookin' that pore ol' Lufkin hit the ice-cream truck. Doin' about forty, too, had to have all those stitches in his forehead."

"I'll be damned," said Benny.

Susan nodded.

Du Pré had his drink and he went behind the bar to fix another.

"Who is it?" said Benny.

"Pidgeon," said Susan. "Surely you remember Pidgeon."

"Oh," said Benny.

"Do you remember Pidgeon, Benny?" said Susan, sweetly.

"Sure," said Benny, looking innocent.

"So that is why Lufkin wrecked the patrol car," said Susan.

"Oh, hell," said Benny. "That's nothin'." He stood up and put on his hat.

"Nothing?" said Susan.

Benny shook his head.

"Nope," he said.

Susan looked at him.

"Remember when I ran the tractor through the side of the barn and took out the old jeep, the baler, the harrow, and the barn, too?" said Benny.

Susan looked at him.

"Well," said Benny, edging backward, "Pidgeon was out by our place there talking with Harvey and Du Pré and she dropped something and bent over to pick it up."

And Benny ran through the front door.

"See," said Susan Klein, looking at the door, "why I love that guy?"

CHAPTER

27

"So you have this dinner with Pidgeon," said Du Pré, "and she says she is loving Bart. She is drunk, yes?"

Madelaine nodded and she sipped her fizzy pink wine.

"Hard to tell who loves what," she said, looking at Du Pré.

"Bart is terrified," said Du Pré.

"Pidgeon isn't," said Madelaine. "It is that Pallas who digs out the news from that Pidgeon and says, well, you have dinner with Madelaine, tell her, we help you out."

Du Pré nodded.

"I am glad she is some few thousand miles away," said Du Pré. "Little shit is scary."

"So," said Madelaine, "Pallas is getting everything in order. She helps Pidgeon."

"Ripper," said Du Pré.

"Even up," said Madelaine. "None of you fools ever had one chance."

"Not even his teeth help," said Du Pré.

"Pallas knock them out of his head, tell him get his ass down the dentist and get some better ones. Pallas, she does not waste words or time ver' much."

"So you are there, Bart is calling," said Du Pré.

"Bart can't call," said Madelaine. "Him froze up like deer, the headlights. I have to punch in the numbers, say, hi, Pidgeon, got that dumb shit here, wants to talk to you, here."

"What does Bart say," said Du Pré, looking up at the ceiling.

"Gurk," said Madelaine. "He say that a few times."

"Gurk?" said Du Pré.

"Gurk," said Madelaine.

"So him gurking away," said Du Pré. "They decide anything?"

"Sort of," said Madelaine.

Du Pré nodded.

"Bart, him gurking, me, I take the telephone away, tell Pidgeon he is sending the plane for her, be there soon, we will call back, tell her when to be there, meet it. I hang up, beat on Bart, him call, plane is on its way, Bart goes home, hide under the bed."

"OK," said Du Pré.

"He is a nice man," said Madelaine. "Me, I think Pidgeon is ver' right. They both ended up with too much and so they can complain about it to each other, give them something to do."

Susan Klein shook on her stool behind the bar.

"How your legs?" said Madelaine.

"Get both your Achilles tendons cut," said Susan, "it is never quite the same. I just can't stand for very long."

"Go home," said Madelaine. "I stay and close up."

Susan had had ripples of pain going across her forehead for an hour.

"You sure?" said Susan.

"Yah," said Madelaine.

Susan limped off and they heard the back door open and close and then her pickup's engine started and she went off.

There was no one else in the bar.

"You," said Madelaine, "go out, see about that dumb shit under the bed. Pidgeon won't be too offended if he gets drunk, but Bart will torture himself for a month, you know."

Du Pré nodded.

He drove out to Bart's ranch and he parked and got out and went in to find Bart and Booger Tom at the kitchen island drinking coffee. Bart kept shaking his head.

"I tol' him to take a couple horses and head fer the deep back country," said Booger Tom.

"No, no," said Bart. "I am very happy. I never dreamed she would have any use for me at all."

"No accountin' for taste," said Booger Tom. "Especially when it is so damned atrocious."

"Thank you," said Bart.

"That girl's as pretty as a new calf in a field of clover," said Booger Tom.

"I hadn't," said Bart, "thought of it that way."

He looked at Du Pré.

"No," said Bart, "I won't. And thank Madelaine for me."

Du Pré nodded.

"I got a couple things to do, the shop," he said.

He went out and across the big ranch yard to the long, low metal building that held the tools and benches for working on the ranch machinery. Du Pré went through and out the back door and across the pasture to a small stone and wood building, built very low to the ground, out in a dish in the earth.

He took a key out of his pocket and he unlocked the door and he left it sitting open and he went down the six steps to the small room where the dynamite was kept. There was a plastic box under a bench and Du Pré pulled it out and he took off the lid and grabbed two blocks of explosive. He put the lid back and he put the blocks in an old plastic grocery bag, and then he found some fuses and caps in the drawers of a cabinet set on the bench.

He put the fuse in the bag and the caps in his shirt pocket and he went back out and he closed and locked the door and he went back to the machine shop and put the key back on its nail and then he went to the house.

Bart and Booger Tom were still at the kitchen island, and they both looked up when Du Pré came in.

"We figure," said Booger Tom, "we just go in over the horns. Bart will go to that race in South Dakota, we'll take Tomás, and see what comes up in the stew."

Du Pré nodded.

"It is the only way," said Bart. "We can just sort of chaff Blackmore for hangin' Tomás on us, should raise his blood pressure a few points."

Du Pré nodded.

"So what do you think?" said Bart.

"Good," said Du Pré. "There will be very many people there and so not much could happen, and then if we are right they will be raided not long after the race, so there will be people there, Ripper, him already there."

"Good," said Booger Tom. "I thought you'd have some pissant objection."

Du Pré shook his head.

"Two weeks," said Bart. "I wonder if I can get the lovely Pidgeon to stay home."

Du Pré shrugged.

"I am sure glad," said Booger Tom, "I got my own house."

"I hadn't thought of that," said Bart.

"I live at Madelaine's anyway," said Du Pré, "so no problem for me."

Bart looked round the house. There were valuable paintings on the walls and expensive furnishings.

"She'll want to change it all, won't she?" he said.

"They generally do," said Booger Tom. "She'll pee in all the corners soon as she gets here."

Bart nodded.

"Well," he said, "I guess it is time for me to drive down to the Billings Airport. She'll be in in a few hours."

"It has been nice knowin' ya," said Booger Tom.

Bart looked at the old cowboy.

"Du Pré," he said, "take this old bastard out back and shoot him, will you?"

CHAPTER

28

"I been hearing about that shit for a long time," said Buddy Devlin. "So you tell me what I kin do."

Du Pré ran through it.

"At first light," said Buddy. "Tell you what. I got some tundra tires still, from when I was a bush pilot in Alaska, 'fore Dad died. Hell with the strip. You may have more folks around than you want. What say we just take a little trip over there and a look-see. All I would need with them is some pasture. Hell, even a meadow would do in a pinch. This little bird rakes up the air."

Du Pré nodded.

"Way I figure," said Buddy, "all we could get accused of is unlawful possession of explosives, malicious destruction of property, breaking and entering, and bad manners. Shit, we kin handle that."

"He is crazy," said Du Pré. "Me, I do not want him to use them planes first, you know."

"That'd be good," said Buddy.

"I have not been in there," said Du Pré, "but planes, they are there and if I go in and the law, they screw around, maybe Blackmore, him get out with one of them."

"Oh, I know, I know," said Buddy, "I went to a horse sale down to Wyoming 'bout six months back, and there was one of them meetings later, and I stayed about five minutes. Hear them tell it, the country is about to be overrun with Commies and the government is after them all personally. 'Course, way they go on and the crap they have lyin' around, I would hope the government *is* after them all personally, myself."

"So," said Du Pré, "when you want to do this?"

Buddy looked at the sky. There was a line of clouds on the far western horizon and a few fluffy gobs of white sailing past overhead.

"We kin be down there and back in three hours," said Buddy, "with time to look it over. Let's just go. Marge will make up some sandwiches and we'll take us a jug of lemonade and just go see what ol' Ferris has got by way of a place to pick you up."

Buddy went off to the house and he was soon back with a paper sack and a gallon jug. Marge, his Chinese wife, came along, her arms folded against the rising wind.

"Hi, Du Pré," she said, smiling. She had a lovely round face, and Du Pré smiled back.

"Madelaine asks about you," said Du Pré.

"I keep meaning to get over there," said Marge. "But you know how it is. You have twenty things to do in a day and by noon it is up to forty."

"The romantic western life," said Buddy.

They went to the little plane and got in and Buddy started the engine and waited for the carburetor to warm.

"She's a little old," said Buddy, over the engine's racket, "but I have had her apart about forty times and I know her real good."

The little plane bounced down the dirt strip and clawed into

136

the air quickly and Buddy pulled the plane in a wide circle to gain altitude.

He set course and adjusted the prop pitch and they droned across the sky. Du Pré could see the plane's shadow going over the land below.

Forty-five minutes later they could see the island range of mountains that Blackmore's ranch was set against, and Buddy turned to Du Pré and he grinned.

"I thank you fer thinkin' of me," he said. "I wanted to do something but I had no idea what. Hell, I hope my taxes go fer education, but folks like Blackmore are proof against it, I guess."

Du Pré laughed.

"Damn it," said Buddy. "These old boys set around worryin' about things that aren't there and gearing up to kill folks that are. That plane you were talking about was a little before my time."

"Mine, too," said Du Pré. "Me, I look it up. P-38 Lightning, maybe, twin engine, very fast, very powerful, carries big payload, very heavy armed."

"Could make a real big mess, I guess," said Buddy.

Du Pré nodded.

"That's it, ain't it?" said Buddy, pointing.

"No," said Du Pré. "That is the little place. The big one is around that mountain, there."

Buddy nodded and he took the plane down slowly and they came round the peak of the mountain and an updraft lifted them suddenly a few hundred feet.

"Whee," said Buddy. "This thing is made of the best toothpicks and tinfoil—'case you was wondering."

Blackmore's main ranch appeared suddenly, and the airstrip was very stark against the land, a long double strip set against the west winds.

"Lot of strip for a ranch," said Buddy, "and see there . . . I think part of it is concrete . . . been nubbled and painted, I bet. See, the grass is movin' either side but not on it."

Du Pré squinted.

"I can't see it," he said.

"Poor old fart," said Buddy. "Well, what I think is this. At first light, you set the fuse to give you three, four minutes, and I'll touch down halfway down the strip, you dive in, and off we go."

"OK," said Du Pré. "There is no place within ten miles I can hide a car, get to it and be gone. Not many roads, no cover much."

"I see that," said Buddy. "Let's go and look over there."

He took the plane down to a gleam of water a couple of miles west of the main ranch house. Cut stumps of trees lay like white circles on a brown field.

"It had some help," said Buddy. "Blackmore is so paranoid he did this. Probably why he bought the damned place. Good fields of fire in all directions and no cover for the enemy."

"I get dropped off, walk in," said Du Pré.

"I bet you one shiny new quarter he's got all sorts of electronic shit will see you right off," said Buddy.

"Maybe," said Du Pré.

"Tell you what," said Buddy. "There ain't no maybe about it. You would probably get your ass shot. No, there has got to be a better way."

"Me, I do not know what it would be," said Du Pré.

"Du Pré," said Buddy, "this one is a little big for the likes of us. What happens, you just swear you seen the damn plane and some illegal weapons and let the Feds have it."

Du Pré looked off at the western horizon.

"Maybe," he said.

"It won't work," said Buddy.

Du Pré nodded.

"This Blackmore, he does them brush races a lot, right?" said Buddy.

"Yah," said Du Pré.

"So happens," said Buddy, "I got a cousin who works for ATF. I know him real well."

Du Pré nodded.

"The government isn't all bad," said Buddy.

Du Pré looked at him.

"They'll just fuck it up," said Buddy. "But then, it is *their* problem."

CHAPTER

29

Madelaine and Susan were bustling around the saloon dusting and cleaning and Jacqueline came in with a huge box of flowers cut from the big garden she kept.

Du Pré sat at the bar.

"You could do something useful," said Susan.

Madelaine snorted.

"You let Du Pré touch the flowers, they will turn black," she said. She smiled sweetly at Du Pré.

"I am hunter," said Du Pré, "not gatherer."

Madelaine and Susan looked at each other.

"Does he know?" said Susan.

Madelaine shook her head.

"I'm not telling him," said Susan.

Du Pré finished his drink and he got up.

"Me," he said, "I probably do not want to know. It would be too much."

"They will be here in an hour or so, we are having a party," said Madelaine.

"No shit," said Du Pré. "All along I think this is for haying crews coming in when it is hot for beer."

"Ver' funny," said Madelaine.

"Bart might be a lot happier," said Susan.

"Bart don't know how, be happy," said Du Pré, "unless he is digging, hole in the ground with his backhoe, that dragline. Bart, him ver' happy digging holes."

"Pidgeon will be good for him," said Madelaine.

"The others," said Susan, "were not. Poor Bart."

"I am glad, his life it is all straight, out ahead," said Du Pré. "If he did not make it to the airport, maybe."

"He made it," said Susan.

"We make sure he does," said Madelaine.

"Oh," said Du Pré.

"So," said Madelaine, "why don't you take the big broom, go hunt crap on the front porch?"

Du Pré fetched the big push broom and the flat broom and he went out and he brushed the leaves and dirt and dust from the porch flooring, and he used the flat broom to get the crud in the corners. He looked up the street when light flashed on glass.

Bart's big green SUV, one of them anyway.

Tinted windows.

Du Pré went back inside with the brooms.

"Him here," said Du Pré. "I got get my tuba, play 'God Save the Bart' or something."

The room looked wonderful. There were vases of gladiolas and lilies on each table and one huge bowl of mixed blossoms on the bar.

The door opened and Pallas came in. She blinked for a moment and she looked round the room.

"Who fucked this dog?" she said. And she grinned.

"Oh," said Du Pré.

"He didn't know," said Madelaine, smirking at Susan.

Pallas went to Du Pré and she hugged him.

"Hi, Gran'père," she said. "I leave Baltimore on fire."

Du Pré laughed.

The door opened again and Pidgeon came in, dressed in simple clothing, a silk blouse and slacks and cowboy boots. She looked stunning. Bart came in right after her, looking sheepish.

Madelaine and Susan went to Pidgeon, and all of them hugged and kissed each other.

"So you are here," said Madelaine.

"Yup," said Pidgeon. "Finally got some nerve."

Bart came up behind her and put a hand round her waist and she leaned against him.

"What him say when Pallas, she is there?" said Madelaine.

"I said, '*Oh, shit!* Nice to see you,'" said Bart. "What else is there to say?"

"She was homesick," said Pidgeon.

Pallas grinned.

"Bad," she said. "Miss the sagebrush, the cowshit, my brothers and sisters."

"They almost got all the stitches out now," said Madelaine. "You behave."

"I am going, see Lourdes," said Pallas.

"She will be by here," said Madelaine, "about five minutes."

They heard horse hooves on the street outside.

"That is Stewball, going to meet her, the school," said Madelaine.

Pallas grinned and she ran out.

Bart looked at the beautiful woman he had on his arm.

He looked stunned and disbelieving.

Du Pré turned aside to laugh.

"You got another name, besides Pidgeon?" said Madelaine. "I never know it."

Pidgeon nodded.

"Samantha," she said. "Little Samantha Pidgeon from San Diego. I never quite felt like a 'Samantha' but I kinda like Sam."

"You quit the FBI?" said Madelaine.

Pidgeon shook her head.

"Leave of absence," she said. "I was planning on just doing consulting work for 'em anyway. I kinda don't get on that well with the paper pushers. We got one who's overwhelmed by the size of his new desk and especially his office and he does like lots of paper pushed, so I told him to shove it. Harvey talked me out of resigning and the new droid out of firing me, which is what I was really hoping for, so here I am."

"Hungry?" said Madelaine.

"Starving," said Pidgeon.

They went to the bar and sat and Susan went back to cook up some cheeseburgers and fries and the four of them sat looking at each other and then they all broke down laughing.

The door opened and Booger Tom limped in, using his cane today, and he gimped up to Pidgeon and he bent down a little to stare a bit closer at her tits.

"Same ones," he said. "I recall now."

"Good to see ya," said Pidgeon, "ya goddamned old goat."

Booger Tom nodded.

Madelaine went behind the bar and mixed up a ditch for the old cowboy.

He nodded and sipped and nodded again.

The smoky mirror in the backbar held their faces softened and dark, in a rippled night.

Pidgeon looked round.

"So we are all going to the race in South Dakota, I expect," she said.

"Yes," said Bart. "It is the only way."

"Where's this Mexican kid, Tomás Guerrero?" she said. "School, I hope."

"He's there," said Madelaine.

Pidgeon nodded.

143

"Bad bunch of people," she said.

Booger Tom sipped his drink.

"That they are," said the old cowboy, "and a-gettin' worse."

Bart put a hand to his mouth. He stifled a yawn.

"C'mon, hon," said Pidgeon, getting down from the stool.

She took Bart's arm and they went out.

"What does that gorgeous woman want with that damned fool?" said Booger Tom.

Everybody made rude farting noises.

The old cowboy grinned.

CHAPTER

30

"No shit," said Harvey.

"That is what she tell me, what is maybe down there," said Du Pré into the phone. "Buddy said he had a cousin, ATF, would call him."

"Oh, God," said Harvey. "Not them. Please, God, not them. And if I may ask, why the hell are you calling me? I know you. You would have taken care of it."

"It is my government," said Du Pré. "Something needs to be done, I think of them first off."

"So you couldn't get in there," said Harvey. "Makes sense. Blackmore'd have sensors all over the place, if he has got that plane there."

"She tell me it has a double body, the back," said Du Pré.

"Twin booms," said Harvey. "Pretty much couldn't be anything else. Still isn't enough to get a warrant. You having a drink with an alcoholic cook. Nope, not even the most forbearing judge would like that one. Nope. Not even in our present state of patriotism and readiness would a judge like that one."

"Pidgeon is here," said Du Pré.

"At last," said Harvey. "The poor girl was pining for that guinea idiot for fucking *years . . .* and he is going to be one very happy boy he knows what is good for him. She'll tell him what's good for him. Pidgeon has a terrifyingly good brain, and she wouldn't hide it. The bureaucrats liked her about as well as they did their piles. I will have to spend a good deal less time keeping her from harm, that is for sure. To make things perfect, they gave me some little Harvard dink who spends his free time saving endangered doodlebugs. He isn't all bad. He said he went into the study of assholes because he hates all mankind and they were a lot he could in good conscience eliminate."

"Oh," said Du Pré.

"He will be less trouble than Pidgeon," said Harvey. "If I can keep him away from weapons of mass destruction. I fear Geoffrey would be sorely tempted to use them."

"So," said Du Pré. "It is that we all are going, that South Dakota race, even that Mexican kid we pick up."

"Makes sense," said Harvey.

"Pidgeon she go with Bart, Bart explain Tomás, Stewball wins the race. So then what?" said Du Pré.

"Those three guys you photographed," said Harvey, "if they are there, which I doubt, we would like to know. Our good Limey friends would like to know even more."

"Very nice," said Du Pré. "English and Irish been killing each other a thousand years, they probably don't know what else to do. What I am asking, though, is what is this, this race, what happens at it?"

Harvey was silent.

"Probably not much," he said finally. "Look, we are a lot looser than we were before those demented wogs smashed the planes into the World Trade Center and the Pentagon. I'll see about

146

going in after Blackmore's toy there while he's off watching the race. These brush races get used to wash money. They pay out cash, unless there are cops on the way, then they just bolt and send large checks. But the money that comes in isn't the money that goes back out. There will be three, four million bet on this race in South Dakota, we hear, and that is a lot of hundred dollar bills don't have a tail on them."

"And some of it comes out is not good money," said Du Pré.

"Yup," said Harvey. "All over the world very gifted folks are trying to make hundred-dollar bills as good as the ones they print at the Treasury. If enough of those phony notes get pumped into the American economy, we got troubles. Of course, all those countries where our money is prized have worse problems. Russia, for instance. They wipe their asses with rubles, them Russian crooks. They like American C-notes."

"Me, I think it is these patriot nuts," said Du Pré. "So it is more this other thing."

"Blackmore and the fellows he plays with haven't got enough brains to stuff one olive apiece," said Harvey. "No, what happens to them is they have some guy show up can use a typewriter and a computer and address an envelope and keep the books and whose English is perfect for writing calls to action and explanations of how the International Jewish Conspiracy owns everything, and is personally going to steal every cow those dumb bastards have. They like the guy, because he can spell and shit, and so they tell him everything they know, which is never that much, and then the guy busts them, on account he is one of us. They never learn. If anyone shows up who can spell, he has to be an FBI agent. You would think that they would have figured that out by now, but they just never do."

"You just go get that plane," said Du Pré. "I read about them, they carry a ton and a half, and that is a lot of belts of ammunition."

"Yes," said Harvey, "it is."

"Blackmore, him say there is a surprise, this race, he don't say more," said Du Pré.

"Could mean a lot of things," said Harvey. "I would not think it would be bad, on account of the fellows come bet on the race are folk Blackmore likes, and as stupid as he is. No, I doubt there is much to it. A new video, that's it. They love making videos."

"OK," said Du Pré. "You know that Pallas is here."

"Yeah," said Harvey. "Jean and I took the pair of them to the airport to meet the plane Bart sent for them. Baltimore is not having sleepless nights anymore. Yeah, Ripper is out there already, him and his teeth. That guy has a very warped sense of humor. Remember he went on that one raid dressed as the Mad Hatter?"

"Yah," said Du Pré.

"He got the roof on one once, came down through the skylight in a gorilla suit," said Harvey.

"Ver' funny guy," said Du Pré.

"No good sense," said Harvey.

"Him get killed," said Du Pré.

"Nope," said Harvey. "One would think so, but he will not. No, Ripper was the sole survivor of that bunch of kids went down the Amazon. A nuke could take out Washington, here, and when the dust settled, Ripper would pop up along with the cockroaches and not a scratch on him. No, he is one of those that has that crazy light around him, like Crazy Horse."

"Pallas worries him," said Du Pré.

"Pallas," said Harvey, "worries God Almighty. No, not even Ripper could survive her. You're right."

"Who is there, besides Ripper?" said Du Pré.

"A few folks," said Harvey. "I got the leaker here narrowed down to three people. Probably bust her before the race, things go right."

"Her?" said Du Pré.

"Sure," said Harvey. "Equal opportunity means just that. No, it is one of three women here. Dunno which, but I know it is one of them. Case you were interested, most of the mob hits women do now. They look so sweet and innocent. Pushing the baby carriage with the two Tech-9s in it. Actually, they use silenced twenty-twos like any pro."

"OK," said Du Pré.

"You see the old man lately?" said Harvey.

"Benetsee?" said Du Pré. "Sweat with him a while back."

"Spooky old bastard," said Harvey. "I knew about twelve of them when I was growing up, there on the Rez."

"So," said Du Pré. "You have told me not much."

"Whaddya want?" said Harvey. "Confessions?"

"Madelaine says come and dance," said Du Pré.

"Soon," said Harvey. "Soon's I find the leaker."

"I will tell her that," said Du Pré.

"You maybe warn Ripper?" said Du Pré.

"Nah," said Harvey. "Fuck him." And he hung up.

CHAPTER

31

Du Pré woke early and saw the pale light rising and he got up from the bed that Madelaine lay in and he went to the window and he looked out and he saw a feather fluttering in the easy wind.

He pulled on his clothes and boots and he walked out of the back door and around to the side of the house to the lilac bush. A single feather, black, a crow's, that had been dipped in white paint.

"Old Man," said Du Pré. "You are here, come now."

There was no answer. Du Pré nodded, went back in the house, scribbled a note to Madelaine, and he went out to his old cruiser and he started it and he drove out to the old man's shack. He could see a white plume of smoke from the road, rising up behind the cabin, from the trench where the stones were heated for the sweat lodge.

Du Pré parked in the best ruts the drive had to offer and he walked around the cabin and down the short drop to the creek's little flood plain, where the sweat lodge stood.

Benetsee was watching the stones heat. They were sitting on crisscrossed stacks of pitch pine that was burning fiercely. When the wood was sufficiently consumed, the heavy stones would fall through the char, hot enough to make steam in the sweat lodge.

The old man stood with his back to Du Pré. When he turned Du Pré gave a start.

Benetsee wore paint on his face, half of it yellow, the other half black, white spots on cheek and forehead where the black covered his old skin.

The stones began to drop and Du Pré took a steel shovel and he carried them one by one to the sweat lodge, setting them in the trench just to the right of the door.

"Plenty," said Benetsee, when the sixth stone, the size of a small watermelon, had been laid in the slit earth.

They both stripped and got in and Du Pré pulled the flap down behind him. He sat with his hands on his knees. Benetsee poured a dipper of water on the rocks that glowed faint purple in the dark and white billows of steam erupted and the sweat lodge grew close and very hot.

Benetsee started to sing, a song Du Pré did not know, in a language he could not place.

The song had a chorus and he sang with the old man after the third time he had heard it.

Benetsee stopped singing abruptly and he yelled and the yell rose in volume until Du Pré's ears crackled with too much noise, and then the old man went past on all fours, through the flap and Du Pré followed him, and when he at last wiped enough sweat away from his burning eyes so he could see, he staggered to the bank of the creek and he plunged into the long deep pool of water. It was cold and it felt wonderful.

His heart hammered for a moment and then calmed.

The water rippled, full of light.

The old man was floating downstream ten feet or so, his weirdly painted face barely out of the water.

Du Pré was so hot his head was still running sweat, even though he had plunged into the water. He ducked under and shook his head and water bubbled in his nostrils. He came up and he stroked to shore, just three pulls, and he grabbed a willow trunk and he pulled himself out of the water.

There were old towels on tree limbs and Du Pré dried himself and he put his clothes and boots back on.

Benetsee appeared suddenly, as he always did, stepping out of the thick willows clothed now in leather. His pants had bone pegs on the outer seams and his tunic was covered with porcupine-quill embroidery, and he had put three eagle feathers in his hair. They sat to the left, pointing down, three enemies killed.

Du Pré suddenly felt weak and dizzy and he dropped to his knees, putting out his hands and breathing deeply. His vision broke into gold-and-black dots and he moaned.

Then it cleared, he felt better, he got up.

The old man was gone.

"God damn you!" yelled Du Pré.

The fires that Benetsee had set under the stones were low, no smoke rising, just a shimmer of heat above the pit.

A kingfisher flew past, said *skraaak!* and was gone, a black and blue and white dart.

Du Pré went back to his cruiser and he opened the door and he sat with his boots on the ground.

He reached under the seat for his flask. It wasn't there.

"Fucking old thief!" he said.

He had another bottle in the trunk of the cruiser. He opened it and he had a long pull and he sat until he felt right.

Then he drove back to Madelaine's.

She was in the backyard, eating a muffin and drinking strong black coffee.

The black feather still danced on its thread.

Du Pré went into the house and he got a couple muffins from

the pan and he poured himself coffee and he went out to the little plank table.

"Old bastard," said Du Pré.

"Him worried," said Madelaine.

"Me, too," said Du Pré. "I do not want, take Lourdes to this race. It is too dangerous."

Madelaine looked down at her cup.

"Got to," she said. "Otherwise you have to make excuse."

"Stewball pull a tendon," said Du Pré.

"Maybe," said Madelaine. "But they let you in to bet."

"Maybe," said Du Pré.

"Tomás has been making calls," said Madelaine. "Harvey, him tell Tomás what to say, so you could do that."

Du Pré nodded.

"These ver' bad people, Du Pré," said Madelaine. "So maybe it is good she goes. Maybe that Harvey, the others, come on in while they are watching the race."

"It is not very long," said Du Pré. "If they are watching from the time the riders take their horses, the gates, seven or eight minutes."

"Long time," said Madelaine.

"OK," said Du Pré. "But me, I want, talk that Harvey."

Madelaine nodded.

"But we could all go, too," she said. "You know, Pidgeon, Bart, Pallas, Lourdes, you, Booger Tom."

"People are maybe getting killed," said Du Pré.

"*Non,*" said Madelaine. "I don't think so maybe. Maybe it will not be like that."

Du Pré shook his head.

"They don't let you in, that leaves Ripper," said Madelaine. "If they have not figured him out yet."

Du Pré looked at her.

"What Benetsee say?" said Madelaine.

"What him *say?*" said Madelaine, again.

"Him don't say nothing," said Du Pré. "Him just sing a song I don't know."

"What is the song?" said Madelaine.

Du Pré sang it, mumbling the words.

Madelaine laughed.

"Stone Boilers' song," she said.

"Them Assinniboine some fighters," said Du Pré.

"All fighters," said Madelaine. "All sing fighting song."

Du Pré shook his head.

"My grandmother is Stone Boiler," said Madelaine. "They all fight together."

CHAPTER
32

Booger Tom and Lourdes were in the pasture behind Raymond and Jacqueline's house, the house that Du Pré had been raised in and the house he had raised both his daughters in.

The horse looked brightly at Du Pré when he walked through the gate. He snorted and danced a little.

"This goddamn horse," said Booger Tom, "is a ham. He wants an audience when he takes a piss."

"He is a ver' special horse," said Lourdes.

"Don't he know it," said Booger Tom.

The horse's mane was combed, tail shining and without tangles, hooves oiled, and right fetlock wrapped.

"You maybe should sleep in the stall," said Du Pré.

"*Non,*" said Lourdes, "but I sleep, the little hayloft not so far away. I tell him last week he can't come see me, walk me home from school, it is too dangerous, so he does not."

"Hobbles might have had something to do with it," said Booger Tom. Lourdes laughed.

Du Pré put out his hand and he stroked Stewball's soft nose.

"Been eatin' worry beans," said Booger Tom, "ain't you?"

Du Pré nodded.

There was yelling coming from the house.

"The Pallas and Jacqueline heavyweight match," said Booger Tom. "I ain't bettin'. I'm runnin'."

"She wants to come to that race, South Dakota," said Lourdes. "She thinks Ripper is there."

Du Pré nodded.

"Which he probably is," said Lourdes. She smiled at Du Pré, her black eyes very old in her child's face.

Du Pré went back to his cruiser and he got his cell phone out of the case and he dialed and he waited and when the woman answered he said a name.

"Du Pré," said Harvey Wallace.

"OK," said Du Pré. "This, I don't know . . ."

"I do know some things now," said Harvey. "Caught the bitch. She has seventeen years here and you'd think she woulda learned something in that time. The muffled sound is us trying to keep it out of the newspapers until enough maggots climb on the hook."

Du Pré laughed.

"Anybody who gets fundamentalist religion," said Harvey, "oughta resign and go pester the neighbors. On top of that, the dumb bitch has a law degree and she still thinks the Second Amendment gives ordinary citizens the right to keep and bear arms, which it does not, and that God Almighty created the world a few thousand years ago. Where did we get this, fer chrissake?"

"It is too dangerous," said Du Pré.

Harvey was silent for a while.

"I doubt it," he said. "Blackmore won't fly that monster he has hidden underground there, because if he does and it gets spotted, he loses it. He may fly it, but I would expect only at night. No, what we do is this. As soon as the race begins there in South Dakota we land on Blackmore's spread and roll it up. Ripper's in place, all is right with the world, and anyway these folks have always been talk, talk talk."

"Do it sooner," said Du Pré.

"I want all the flies," said Harvey, "in the bottle."

"Plans," said Du Pré. "They are just plans, never work out."

"You don't trust me," said Harvey.

"No," said Du Pré.

"Pidgeon is going, with Bart," said Harvey. "Pidgeon will be all suited up."

"Yah," said Du Pré.

"She'll be ready," said Harvey.

"So," said Du Pré, "I think I don't like this, I do not have to go but everyone else will."

"Yup," said Harvey. "Shame to feel left out and all."

"You lie to me," said Du Pré.

"Only," said Harvey, "when necessary."

Du Pré hung up, he walked back to the house.

Pallas was sitting on the front porch, rocking slowly in the big old green wood rocker Du Pré had found at the dump thirty years before.

The girl looked over at him.

"You worry," she said. "You always worry. You know what this is? These are people, want to kill everybody they don't like, and they don't like us, so we go, say, how is this now?"

Du Pré laughed.

How is this now?

"So we will be all right," said Pallas. "They are not that danger-ous these ones."

"Stupid," said Du Pré, "is dangerous."

"Yeah," said Pallas. "And they all got guns but they can't hit any-thing with them, no?"

Du Pré laughed.

"We go to the race, win the race," said Pallas. "Win the other races, too, you know."

Du Pré took out his tobacco pouch, rolled a smoke, batted the girl's hand away when she reached for it.

"You think I am being dead soon anyway," said Pallas. "So give the last cigarette, eh?"

"You are too young," said Du Pré. "Ver' bad habit."

"When you start smoking, grandpapa?" said Pallas.

"I am seven," said Du Pré.

"Catfoot like that?" said Pallas.

"Catfoot don't know about it," said Du Pré. "Mama, she figure it out, take after me with a belt."

"Your mama hit you?" said Pallas.

Du Pré shook his head. "She don't try hard, catch me, see."

Pallas laughed.

"They are pret' good to me," said Du Pré.

"You are trouble," said Pallas.

"Kids," said Du Pré, "are trouble. They are not trouble they are *dead*."

"You see Benetsee?" said Pallas.

Du Pré nodded.

"Him painted," he said.

"You see that before?" said Pallas.

Du Pré nodded.

"One time," he said. "But it was different. This is a paint for war."

"So," said Pallas, "him come, too."

Du Pré shrugged.

"All together," said Pallas.

Du Pré started to hum the Assinniboine song that Benetsee had sung in the sweat lodge.

All together . . .

He hummed and hummed, and Pallas did, too, and the song rose and fell, vaguely Celtic, but it was not.

Du Pré stopped.

Pallas looked at him.

"We are bait maybe," he said.

CHAPTER

33

Du Pré looked out the window of the pickup. A huge raven sat on
a dead deer, black, old, eerie.

The big bird looked back at Du Pré.

"It is all right, Grandpapa," said Pallas from the back seat. The
pickup was Bart's, the sort that has four doors and two wide seats
and a long bed in the back. The camper in the bed held food and
gear and guns, the trailer behind, Stewball. Lourdes was back
there with the horse.

Booger Tom snorted.

Madelaine took Du Pré's hand.

They drove for four hours and the sun westered. They came to
the turn that led north toward the ranch where the race was to be.

Bart and Pidgeon were in a big green SUV behind, the windows
so black nothing could be seen in the big car's interior.

"Them windows is illegal, I thought, at least in new cars," said Booger Tom.

Pidgeon had flown down to Billings the day before to get it.

"Not like it was," said Madelaine. "Du Pré, you still think it is like it was. Summer, the men, they go out ten, fifteen miles, watch, women and children grow the corn, the men don't let enemies near. Indian blood telling, yes?"

Du Pré laughed.

"You go there, just you and Booger Tom, it is more dangerous. You know, that Lewis and Clark save themselves, take Sacajawea with them. Indians don't think it is a war party, has a woman in it."

"Indians," said Pallas, "jerks, too."

"Lots of jerks around," said Madelaine, looking back at her. "Always. Be plenty here for sure."

"There it is up there," said Du Pré, crouching down a little to look up through the windshield.

The sun glinted on a silver speck moving across the horizon.

And another.

And another.

They drove on in silence.

Booger Tom looked in the rearview mirror.

The SUV's left-turn signal was blinking.

Booger Tom slowed and he turned on a gravel road that crossed the narrow potholed blacktop they had been traveling on.

A post held a stack of painted arrows with the names of ranchers on them and the number of miles to their spreads.

They drove up a long hill and at the top they could see fifty miles north. The hills rolled on, yellow, brown, purple in the distance, the folds green with bushes where there was more water.

The road went down a very long grade and they got to the bottom and saw a small stand of cottonwoods off to the left. There were a pair of black SUVs parked there, and men in blue shirts and black pants and hats sitting on logs or the hoods of the vehicles.

When they got to the top of the next hill a small plane flew very low over them, coming from behind. The pilot wagged his wings as he rose up.

"Prick," said Booger Tom. "Hope it didn't spook Stewball. They do play dirty, these folks."

"Maybe they are just stupid," said Madelaine.

"Anybody works horses would know better," said Booger Tom. "You kin bet it is some flunky of Blackmore's, maybe that goddamned Texan he runs with."

They drove on, over two more hills, and when they crested the last one they saw a roadblock a hundred yards downhill, a steel fence across the roadbed, more black SUVs, four men in blue shirts and black pants and hats.

"The stupid sons of bitches is wearing Sam Browne belts," said Booger Tom. "Goddamned Nazis."

The old cowboy slowed and stopped and he rolled down his window. One of the men in the odd uniforms stood back, his eyes covered by mirrored sunglasses, a submachine gun in his hands.

The man who came to the pickup looked long at Booger Tom and Du Pré, stared hard at Madelaine and Pallas.

He was young, in his twenties, blond, with a hard, stupid face.

His blue shirt had crosses on the collar and both pockets.

"What the hell is going on?" said Pidgeon, behind them. "We came to race a horse. What is this crap?"

She walked past, lovely in fringed calfskin, dyed maroon, high boots, a flowing silk kerchief, and a tall white hat.

"Security," said the blond man who had looked in the pickup.

The men all stared at Pidgeon, who grinned at them.

"Whatcha afraid of?" she said. "Fuckin' niggers?"

They all laughed then.

"We got Stewball," said Pidgeon. "And we mean to whip ass, we do. Now you don't mind, we'd like to go on, get him pastured, watered, and all."

"Just doin' our duty," said the blond man. His mouth went slack as he stared at Pidgeon.

"Get out of the fuckin' way," said Pidgeon. "We got a horse to race. Jesus, I am gonna take ol' Ferris's head off I see him."

"That's Dave Wilson," said the blond man, "an' that trainer Dumas or whatever. Girl's the rider."

"The hell she is," said Lourdes. "I am the rider. She is my sister come to see me race."

The blond man pulled out a portable telephone and he punched in some numbers, turned, walked away.

"We still have to search," he said. "It's the rules."

"Sure," said Pidgeon. "Make it quick, though."

The men looked in the camper, the horse trailer, the SUV.

Booger Tom unlocked the tool chest in the side of the camper and he pulled out the drawers.

Bart and Pidgeon hauled out suitcases and they opened them and one or another of the oddly uniformed men looked at them.

"Oh," said the blond man, holding up a paperback book, a large thick one. "I read this. It's real good."

"Got to know your enemy," said Pidgeon. "The goddamned Zionist Occupation Government . . ."

"Yeah," said the blond man, staring at Pidgeon's tits. "Yeah, you do."

"Wolfie," said another man, "come look at this."

A long dark-green canister with nylon straps around it. Wolfie picked it up. He stared.

Pidgeon went to it, opened one end.

Wolfie looked in the canister.

He fished out a long bar of steel.

"Folding bench," said Pidgeon. "I can take it out if you like."

Wolfie looked at her again. He shrugged, slid the steel bar back in.

"You can go on," he said.

Pidgeon leaned forward, kissed Wolfie on the cheek.

Wolfie flushed. His fellows hooted.

They drove on.

Pallas reached over the seat to Du Pré.

She pointed to a half-full cup of coffee in the holder on the transom.

Du Pré looked at her. He picked up the cup.

Pallas showed him a little silver disc, the size of a dime. She dropped it in the coffee.

"I see him put this there," she said, pointing to the rearview mirror.

Du Pré nodded.

He looked at the land as the truck gained speed.

"Good country, this," he said.

"Very," said Booger Tom.

"Very," said Madelaine.

"Very, very," said Pallas.

CHAPTER

34

The ranch and outbuildings sat on a long, low tongue of land that fell off into two small watercourses, well sheltered from the Great Plains winds. The main house was a huge faux Spanish hacienda, two-storied, the stucco mangy and showing huge blisters where the paint and plaster had been worked away from the walls by frost.

"I done heard about this place," said Booger Tom. "Built by some dumb bastard from New York come out here 'bout 1920, seen a movie or somethin'."

The outbuildings were newer, post-and-beam buildings covered in steel sheeting, white on the walls and blue on the roofs.

There were several hundred cars and pickup trucks parked off in a flat area, one that had been planted in wheat but now was just a big parking lot.

"Damned shame," said Booger Tom. "That'd be good wheat."

A middle-aged man, weathered and gimpy, walked over to the pickup.

"Put yer horse over thar," he said, waving toward a paddock that had a low white stable beside it.

There were three other horses in the paddock.

"Nope," said Booger Tom. "This here is Stewball and he don't much like crowds."

The cowboy stared at Booger Tom for a moment and then he pulled out a cellular phone and he punched in numbers, his eyes slitted, the phone held at arm's length.

"Old age is hell," said Booger Tom. "I was you I'd get me some readin' glasses."

The cowboy grunted and he thumbed a button on the telephone.

" 'Course, you are from Texas ya can't read anyway," said Booger Tom, helpfully.

"I kin read the fine print on yer label," said the cowboy. "One hundred per cent Montana son of a bitch, what it says."

"My mother come from Texas," said Booger Tom. "I shot her soon as I found out, of course. You know how it is."

"God damn!" said the cowboy, looking at the cellular phone.

"I thought you fellers used knots in a rope send messages," said Booger Tom. "You know, them twisty things?"

"Kind I like best has thirteen winds," said the cowboy. "Fits around the neck real good."

Pallas had gotten out of the truck. She plucked the phone out of the cowboy's hand.

"What number?" she said.

"Ought-three-four," said the cowboy. "It's just fer the ranch."

Pallas punched in the numbers.

She handed the telephone to the cowboy.

He put it to his ear and he waited.

"Folks here with some dog food called Stewball," he said. "They says he gets a private room."

The cowboy listened.

"O-kay," he said.

The cowboy pointed to another paddock, set back in a grove of cottonwood trees.

"Good place," he said. "Lots of ticks."

"Thankee kindly," said Booger Tom, starting the engine.

He drove on to the back paddock and he pulled up beside the gate. Pallas opened the door of the trailer and Stewball backed out, on his own.

Lourdes followed, carrying a nosebag. Du Pré opened the gate and Lourdes and Stewball walked in. She put the nosebag on the big horse and sounds of grinding oats came muffled from the canvas.

There was a small shed big enough for two horses at the far end.

Du Pré sauntered over and he went in and looked around.

Clean straw, hay in a manger, a water bowl with a lever a horse would press with its nose to get a drink.

He looked up at the ceiling.

"Where's the monster?" said Ripper. He was draped across the cross members of the trusses.

Du Pré nodded toward the paddock outside.

"You meet ol' Lew?" said Ripper. "Do his blind act with the phone? We borrowed him from the border patrol. He's the worst border patrol agent they have, spends all his time busting the bastards who prey on the Mexicans coming over. Time to time he moseys on down to old Mexico and grabs somebody we really want, brings them back, saves on all of that paperwork."

"Are you here or not?" whispered Du Pré. "We found a microphone the road guard put in the pickup."

"Not here," said Ripper. "Thing you have to know about these people is that they buy all of the goodies but they very seldom can get them to *work*. They have a couple pros they hired but those two guys can't keep up. I am supposed to be off fixing a fence someone cut. I think it was me cut it. Anyway, I trust the monster will not let on she knows me?"

Du Pré nodded.

"She is smarter than me, you," said Du Pré.

"I *know* that," said Ripper.

There was a sound of helicopter rotors, a chopper getting closer and closer. A few cheers came from the biggest barn.

"Now," said Ripper, "I think what we have been really looking for is here."

He let himself down and he went to the door and he shaded his eyes with his hand.

The sounds were close but there was nothing visible.

The sounds were coming from someplace close, someplace right in the direction they could see.

Whock whock whock.

Louder and louder.

Then the machine rose up suddenly out of a hidden cleft in the earth.

Black and menacing, shiny seven-barreled Gatling guns on front mounts, rockets slung under the stubby wings back of the doors.

"Christ," said Ripper, "they do have the goddamned thing. You can't buy one, but with our idiot surplus sales of Pentagon goodies, you can buy all of the parts. Enough parts were sold so there could be three of them, probably just two."

The damn thing looks like a big-ass wasp, Du Pré thought.

People streamed out of the big barn, pointing up and talking fast to each other.

"OK," said Ripper. "Soon as we see the other one, it is rock-and-roll time."

The Apache hovered low, the pilot flew the black machine around the big barn, then he rose up and tipped forward, and the helicopter moved away, dropped out of sight over the hill.

Ripper went through the fence, got on a horse that was tied to a tree branch, rode off.

"Jesus Christ," said Booger Tom. "That looked like a right nasty machine."

Du Pré grunted.

"Let's smoke," said Booger Tom. "We may not get time to later."

CHAPTER

35

Whole steers turned on spits run by whining electric motors.

Giant kettles held beans, there were plastic tubs full of cole slaw and a bar tent awash in beer and liquor.

Young men in black pants and boots, blue shirts and black Sam Browne belts stood at each entrance and exit, by every door in every building.

"They all look stupid," said Pallas. "Really stupid."

Madelaine laughed. So did Lourdes.

Du Pré, Booger Tom, Bart, Pidgeon, and the girls were in a line to get plates and meat and trimmings.

Booger Tom and Du Pré had large whiskeys, Bart a soda, Pidgeon a bottle of mineral water, the girls had lemonade, and Madelaine had somehow found some pink wine.

They got their food and went out of the tent toward the ranks of trestle tables set up near the big barn. A banner, on which a white cross with crude flaming lightning bolts had been painted, flapped in the evening breeze.

Pallas and Lourdes ate quickly, got up, looked at Madelaine.

The three bent their heads together, and after Madelaine whispered something the girls nodded and went off toward the big stable and paddock.

Du Pré raised an eyebrow. Madelaine smiled.

Du Pré rolled a smoke, gave it to Booger Tom, made another for himself, lit it, and handed it to Madelaine for the one puff she liked.

The talk was loud, forced laughter, the anger under it a smoldering fetor of rage and hate.

A tall white-haired man with a very red face wandered among the tables. He wore vestments, the white cross large on the back and a pair on the front, and the lightning bolts.

After a few words at each table, the man raised his hand in a blessing and then he moved on.

In time he came to the table where Du Pré and the others sat, and he smiled in a jolly way.

"The good Lord blesses us and soon the niggers and their Jew allies will be dust, praise Jesus," he said. He looked at Du Pré and Madelaine, raised an eyebrow.

"You Injuns?" he said.

"Yes," said Madelaine, "but we are right in our hearts."

"Bless you," said the man, lifting his hand in benediction.

"This is kinda hard to stomach," said Bart.

"Suck it up, sweetie," said Pidgeon. "We got bidness here."

They all laughed.

Du Pré looked over at the rows of gray portable toilets and he saw Pallas there, standing between two near the end. Pallas made one "come" motion with her hand and then she went into the plastic booth.

Du Pré coughed, nodded at Pidgeon. She bent her head.

169

"Pallas is in the second john, left side, wants somebody," said Du Pré.

Pidgeon got up, bent over, and kissed Bart on the top of his head, and then she sauntered off toward the toilets.

A loudspeaker clicked on.

"The assembly starts in fifteen minutes," said a metallic voice. "Fifteen minutes in the big barn."

The tables erupted in jabber.

Pidgeon came back, walking slowly, hips and fringe swaying. Men stared at her, their women glared at them.

Pidgeon sat down between Madelaine and Bart.

"Anne-Marie warned the girls there is something going on, Ferris has been bragging about killing weasels tonight, or he says killing rats. The man is insane. So the girls are taking the horses as soon as the assembly starts, and getting out."

Du Pré nodded.

"Anne-Marie has been here before. There's a trail that leads to some breaks on the Little Missouri. She has it all planned out, they can hide there, with the horses, they will be near a square butte that has a pink band near the top," said Pidgeon.

"Too much light," said Du Pré. "There is that helicopter, you know."

"I wouldn't worry about it." said Pidgeon. She smiled, white teeth dazzling.

Ripper, thought Du Pré.

The crowd started to move toward the big barn. Booger Tom got up, took a wrapped bundle the size of a lot of money from his jacket.

"Shall we?" he said.

They sauntered toward the big barn, letting others pass them.

Pidgeon put something in her mouth.

The young men in the uniforms were watching the people coming into the barn and staring hard at the stragglers.

When Booger Tom got to the door, he waved the bundle.

"They got them a collection plate in here?" he said.

"Sure do, brother," said the young man in the uniform.

Booger Tom passed, and then Du Pré.

Pidgeon was behind Madelaine. When she got next to the young man in the uniform, she suddenly vomited.

Pidgeon fell to her hands and knees, puking foam.

"Honey!" said Bart.

Pidgeon hacked and heaved some more. Bart handed her a kerchief and Pidgeon got up slowly, wiping her mouth.

"I need my meds," she said weakly.

They walked away toward the green SUV.

Du Pré and Madelaine and Booger Tom went on in. Booger Tom went to a table just to the left of the door and he handed the bundle to a woman with flaming red hair, who said something in a screechy voice, and then she and Booger Tom laughed.

They found chairs near the back of the barn, next to the aisle, and they sat.

Blue banners with the white cross and the lightning bolts hung at the far end of the barn, behind a dais and podium.

Ferris Blackmore came to the podium and he rapped for silence and he began to speak. The sound system rose and fell, his words were distorted.

". . . country is going to hell . . . inferior humans wrecking it . . . lost the way of Jesus . . ."

People clustered around the bank of electronics, fiddling.

Blackmore raised his right hand high, and when he did there was a sound of running feet, and twenty or so of the young men in the odd uniforms burst in doors on either side of the dais.

Each man carried a submachine gun slung round his neck. They trotted to the front and then they broke into groups of five and they raced down the aisles.

They got to the row where Du Pré and Madelaine and Booger Tom sat.

They leveled guns at them.

"Get up!" snarled the young man who was closest.

"Don't point that thing at me, sonny," said Booger Tom. "I'll shove it right up yer ass."

The young man's eyes narrowed.

"Get up," he said again.

CHAPTER

36

Du Pré and Madelaine and Booger Tom were prodded up to the front of the crowd.

Ferris Blackmore glared down at them.

"Traitors!" he screamed, pointing, and the crowd roared.

"Government agents, the bastards," said Blackmore.

"Peckerheads," said Booger Tom. "You was any dumber all you'd need is water twice a month."

"Shut up!" screamed one of the young men, stepping forward.

Blackmore looked at Du Pré, his brow furrowed.

"Where's the woman and that guy?" he said.

The loopy sound system furled his words, folded them to gibberish.

"I'll shoot the bastard myself!" said a man in the front row. He pulled a pistol from his waistband.

"Not without a fair trial!" yelled Ferris Blackmore.

"These people," said Madelaine, "are seriously nuts."

"Yah," said Du Pré.

Blackmore ranted and screamed for an hour while it got dark outside, and from time to time one or another of the young men in uniform would come in, say something to the guard around the podium, who would say something to Blackmore.

"Find the little bitches," said Blackmore, the sound system clear and loud.

The lights all went out suddenly, the barn was plunged into thick dark.

A few people yelped or screamed.

Lighters flared. A few pocket lights shone weak beams in the huge room.

A sudden floodlight shone on Du Pré and Madelaine and Booger Tom. Someone had gotten a big flashlight.

"Where's Harry?" said Blackmore.

"He went to the chopper," someone said.

"Come on," said Blackmore. "Bring these bastards."

Du Pré and Madelaine and Booger Tom were prodded through the door to the left of the stage, out into the cool night.

"Where'd my granddaughter go?" said Blackmore, his face two inches from Du Pré's.

Du Pré shook his head.

The black helicopter rose up then from behind a low shed out in the pasture, and a floodlight shone down on the ground.

Voices crackled on a radio.

"Don't hurt her," said Blackmore. "Kill the others if you want to, but don't hurt my granddaughter."

"Traitors die," said the crackly voice.

"Shit," said Booger Tom. "They can't beat that thing."

The helicopter rose up and up until it was five hundred feet overhead.

The floodlight began to circle on the ground.

It stopped.

Pidgeon was standing there, looking up, and she had something long on her shoulder, and then there was a sudden hiss and a white vapor trail.

"Ohmigod!" said the voice on the radio, and then there was a bloom of yellow fire against the black night and the black machine, and it fell sideways and began to whirl around, and then it hit the earth very hard and blew up, a horrid flower of orange-black flame.

Ferris Blackmore turned to look at Du Pré and Madelaine.

"Lock 'em in the shed," he said. "We'll take the Humvees."

The three were prodded over to a small metal shed and shoved inside and a hasp slid and a lock clicked.

Du Pré struck a match.

The floor was concrete and the walls thick galvanized metal.

Booger Tom kicked a wall, and yelped.

They all smoked for a while.

Time passed. Fifteen, thirty, forty-five minutes.

Then there were sudden loud sounds of helicopters and a loud voice came from above demanding that everyone lie down where they were and put their hands behind their heads.

"Festerfuck," said Ripper, outside the shed.

There was a clip, a wrench, and Ripper cursed. He slammed something against the door.

More sounds of metal tearing.

The hasp slid back, the door came open.

Floodlights stabbed down from above, a dozen of them, and dust and debris swirled up in the rotor wash.

"Come on out and lie down with your hands behind your heads," said Ripper. "It ain't us fine folks at the FBI. Though they have not said so, I do believe it is the ATF. Those fine people that made Waco such a fun thing."

They filed out. A light shone down and Ripper and Du Pré and Booger Tom and Madelaine lay down and put their hands behind their heads.

175

"You kin see," said Booger Tom, "where a feller like Blackmore would get his ideas."

"We live through this," said Ripper, "I will say I am sorry I misunderstood him so very badly and where can I go to sign up and make amends."

Du Pré looked over to his right.

Pidgeon was slowly strolling toward them.

"You," said a voice overhead. "You, woman, get down."

Pidgeon gave them the finger. She held up a badge and it gleamed in the light, flashing.

"Get down or we'll shoot," said the voice.

Pidgeon looked up and grinned.

She sat down, held up both arms with fingers upraised.

There were vehicles coming, and then men in black jumpsuits and body armor began running into the light, stepping round the many bodies facedown in the dust.

Two of them came to Pidgeon. One held his machine gun on her.

"Point your dick elsewhere," said Pidgeon. "I am a federal agent and a woman. I sue, man, do I like to sue assholes."

The other man plucked the badge from her hand.

He gave it back.

"ATF?" said Pidgeon. "You act like it."

"Christ," said the man.

"Homeland security," said Pidgeon. "This is an airport, right?"

There were two hundred blacksuited men scattered round by now.

"It's an abortion clinic," said Pidgeon. "Cracker John Ashcroft is here. You his munchkins?"

Pidgeon got up and she walked over to Du Pré and Madelaine and Booger Tom.

"You're under arrest," said Pidgeon. "Come along quietly."

"Where is that Bart?" said Madelaine.

"In the SUV," said Pidgeon. "I got him trained. When I say sit and stay, he does."

One of the blacksuited men came running over with a short tube that had a shoulder rest and a pistol grip and nothing in the tube.

"Hey," said Pidgeon, walking over. "That fucker's mine. Give over, assholes, there's a deposit on it."

CHAPTER

37

Buses came, the place was searched, the people were herded on to the buses, and then the big machines whined away.

"Goddamn it," said Pidgeon. "That fucking Blackmore ain't here. He's gone after the girls."

Booger Tom was laughing.

"They took all the horses," he said, "the whole damn bunch. They got easy fifty head out there. Blackmore's chasin' after them, he can't catch them, though."

"Maybe," said Du Pré. "But there is that trail, good buffalo trail there, I don't know."

"I'm trying," said Pidgeon. "These assholes won't lend us a chopper."

"Is it possible," said Ripper, "to delay long enough so that perhaps Pallas is gunned down? Just a thought."

Pidgeon looked at him and smiled.

"Yer dead meat," she said. "Either put the Glock in your mouth or don't, but quit whining."

Pidgeon's cell phone chirred. She flipped it open.

"About fucking time, you bastard," she said. "We need a chopper, and we need it now."

She listened.

She handed the phone to Du Pré.

"Big fucking mess," said Harvey. "I smell congressional hearings, I scent blood. Those idiots never said a word to us and we had agents there. I am going to have heads on poles."

"I am worried, the girls," said Du Pré.

"There is a chopper on the way, but it won't be there for an hour at least," said Harvey. "I am doing the best I can. Thing about some great whacking goatfuck like this is nobody will answer the phone and nobody will agree to anything, because they are talking only to their lawyers."

"They never tell you about this?" said Du Pré.

"Nope," said Harvey. "See, in Washington, knowledge is power and since there is so little knowledge to hold on to, they are desperate in all things. Bureaucratic man."

Madelaine snatched the telephone away.

"You, Harvey," she said, "you get us something. Our girls are out there."

She listened.

"But that," she said, "is illegal, I think. Right."

She handed the phone back to Pidgeon, who shut it up, and she said something in a low voice.

Pidgeon went to Ripper.

"I said that a half hour ago," he said.

"So I am a wimp," said Pidgeon.

"It's a great country," said Ripper. "You can repent and then you can make amends and become a new person."

Pidgeon grabbed Bart's hand and she pulled him along, and Du Pré followed and so did Booger Tom and Madelaine and Ripper. She led them toward a chopper that was sitting behind the big barn. It had a man with a machine pistol standing in front of it and a pilot inside and another older man in a wind breaker shouting into a microphone.

Pidgeon walked up to the guard.

The man stiffened.

"He's sick," she said, pointing to Bart. "We have to get him to a hospital."

"What?" said the man.

Pidgeon had a pistol in her hand by then, pointed at the man's head.

"Nice and easy," said Pidgeon. "Paddypaws off the gun there." She undid the clip and pulled the machine pistol away.

"My tits," she said, "work every time."

"What the fuck?" said the older man at the radio.

"Outta my way, pencil neck," said Ripper, grabbing his shoulder and pulling him out the door.

They all got in.

"Jesus," said the pilot, "you won't get away with this."

"Honeybunch," said Pidgeon, "here's the deal. We are actual FBI agents. There are three young girls out there who are being chased by some of these pieces of shit, and I'm not gonna let them die. So we are going after them, Rosebud. *Now*."

The pilot looked at her.

"Well," he said, "we can't have that now, can we." And he began to flip switches and the big machine trembled as the rotors sped up.

"Scramble," he said. "Hang on before some asshole comes with a fucking form I got to sign."

The helicopter rose up and up, and he looked at Pidgeon, who looked at Du Pré, who pointed north.

There was a roar as the jet assists kicked in and the helicopter sped forward.

"Come on up here, Du Pré," said Pidgeon. "I don't know where to tell him to go."

Du Pré looked at the compass.

"Fifteen degrees left," he said, "then go on. How fast this go?"

"Three hundred," said the pilot, "flat out."

"Do six minutes, thirty miles maybe," said Du Pré.

The helicopter shot forward.

The moon had come up, and the land was stark shadows and bright earth.

Du Pré looked down at the land.

There, a pale ribbon, a few feet wide, a mark on the land a million hooves had made, the buffalo now gone to ghosts, but there it was.

It wandered here and there as they do, for buffalo cannot see ahead, only to the sides.

Tacking back and forth like hairy boats.

"That is it, that ribbon," said Du Pré. "We are looking for headlights, the people who are chasing the girls."

"With the moon they won't need them," shouted the pilot.

The helicopter slowed and hovered.

"Find the horses," said Madelaine, her voice loud. "We get between them and those bastards."

"Ten miles maybe," said Du Pré. "That second hill there . . ." and he pointed.

The pilot nodded.

His radio crackled.

"Return to the ranch, Smitty," said the voice, "or you ain't gonna work here no more."

"Eat my shorts," said Smitty, shutting off the radio.

An emergency light began to flash.

"Just trying to get through," said Smitty.

"They are mad," said Du Pré.

"Oh, how dreadful," said Smitty, "that they would be mad."

"Check that," said Du Pré.

Smitty turned the radio back on.

"You will be shot down if you don't comply," said the voice.

"Oh, balls," said Smitty. "We aren't the enemy."

"We mean it," said the voice. "You are approaching a sensitive area."

181

"The cold war is over," said Smitty.

"True," said the voice, "but the vice president is there shooting pheasants."

"Now?" said Smitty.

"Yeah," said the voice. "They raise them in pens. I don't know if they fly or not."

CHAPTER

38

"They are there," said Du Pré. He pointed down and ahead.

Thirty horses raced down the old buffalo trail, three of them carrying riders.

"This have a speaker?" said Du Pré.

The pilot nodded, handed a microphone over.

"It's on," said the pilot.

The helicopter dipped down and hovered.

"It is me, Du Pré," said Du Pré. "You turn the horses, stop, I will come down."

The girls moved ahead of the horses and began to turn them. The chopper pilot set the machine down on a flat place a half mile away.

Du Pré and Madelaine got out.

"I don't ride horses much," said Pidgeon. " 'Sides, it will be fun to go back and yell at the competition."

The pilot held up a thumb, rose up, and headed south very quickly.

There was a whoosh overhead and a warplane shot past, crossed the moon rising.

The buffalo trail stretched ahead in the moonlight. In five minutes Du Pré and Madelaine could see the milling cavvy of horses, and in five more Pallas and Lourdes and Anne-Marie were standing, holding on to the reins of their mounts.

Stewball whuffled.

"He likes this," said Lourdes.

"Blackmore maybe got away. He was coming after you, a Humvee, maybe two or three, we could not see them go," said Du Pré.

"Take this tack, Grandpapa," said Lourdes. "Me, Pallas, ride bareback. She has a good horse."

They switched the funny pancake saddles and the bits and bridles to fresh horses.

"You know this place, where rich men come, shoot pheasants?" said Du Pré to Anne-Marie.

She nodded.

"It's about ten miles ahead," she said. "But if we go due west we come to the upstream breaks on the Little Missouri. The trail is rough, I don't think they can come on with those Humvees."

She mounted and so did the others, and they clucked and yelled and the horses began to move, not so fast this time.

They came to some closely folded land, steep, where the trail wound down and then up, and then a broad flat stretch a couple of miles wide, and then they began to wind back and forth down a slope to a wind-cut basin.

The horses smelled water and they neighed and whickered, and the pace picked up, and then they came to the Little Missouri, a pale stream a few feet wide, sliding past weird lumps of clay and rock, *malpais,* badlands.

The horses drank and Du Pré and Madelaine and the girls did the same upstream. The water was faintly bitter with alkali.

"It is not enough to make you sick," said Du Pré.

It was getting cold. They gathered sticks and then Pallas whistled.

There was a rick of sticks ten feet high and a hundred feet long, jammed into an overhang.

"What makes these piles?" said Anne-Marie. "I have seen others."

"Wood rats," said Madelaine. "They been working on this pile a hundred years easy."

"Wood rats," said Anne-Marie.

"Wood rats," said Madelaine. "People come here to hunt, they look for a good pile of wood rat sticks, make the fires dry the meat from the buffalo."

They started a fire and sat close.

"How come you three run with all the horses?" said Madelaine.

"My grandfather is crazy," said Anne-Marie, "and he was saying he was going to shoot all of the horses, that there were traitors coming and the horses were traitors, too, and he was going to kill them all. So I found Pallas and Lourdes and we thought we could save them. The gates were all open for some reason. We just rode off like we were exercising our mounts and then we just rallied the others and left like that. No one noticed right away, I guess, and we went as fast as we could."

She began to cry silently, tears forming and slipping down her cheeks.

Madelaine went over to her, took her in her arms. Anne Marie sobbed and sobbed.

"She comes back with us," said Lourdes.

"Right," said Pallas.

Lourdes began to sing then, her clear alto rising up, an old Celtic melody. Pallas joined her, and then so did Anne-Marie.

The song was haunting, old, a lament.

"I play that," said Du Pré. "It is 'The Tears of the Harp.' "

"Found it on one of your records," said Lourdes. "Sort of song you hear once and know forever."

A lament for lost soldiers, Du Pré thought.

185

"Where you learn Gaelic?" said Madelaine. "Pretty good Gaelic, that."

"Internet," said Lourdes. "I am talking the daughter of some old drunk plays fiddle, those little Irish bagpipes, Dublin."

"It is our song," said Anne-Marie.

Du Pré laughed.

"Yes," he said.

These women will not have it another way, not now.

So where is that bastard Blackmore?

Du Pré walked back up the trail and then he got up on a short butte and he walked south, one ear to the wind.

Nothing.

No engine whine or tire sounds.

No lights, but they don't need lights.

He pulled out his pistol, checked the chamber, felt for the other clips, they were there.

Wish that I had a rifle.

Wish I had Catfoot's MP-40.

Du Pré sat all through the night, listening, smoking with his hand cupped around the glowing end of his cigarette.

Nothing came up the trail, nothing flew overhead.

When the light rose up in the morning they stretched and yawned and drank and got mounted.

"We go back," said Du Pré, "they maybe have everything sorted out by now."

They rode back, the horses moving swiftly, but it was not until well past noon that they came over the rise and saw the ranch and the ranked rows of cars and pickups below.

There were a few men in black jumpsuits guarding the place.

When they got to the pasture Du Pré looked over and he saw Harvey walking along, hands in his pockets, a couple of younger agents with him.

The girls and Madelaine carried the tack off.

Harvey stood with his arms on the top rail of the fence, looking off in the distance.

"Good morning," he finally said.

"Yah," said Du Pré. "You find Blackmore?"

"No," said Harvey. "They didn't. They found the two Humvees not far away. Blackmore slipped off, he did, so . . ."

"The plane?" said Du Pré.

"Wasn't there," said Harvey. "Not where you said it was. Nothing there but a very expensive underground hangar. No plane, no tools, no ammunition."

"Pidgeon?" said Du Pré.

Harvey jerked a thumb over his shoulder, toward the main ranch house.

"We will take Anne-Marie with us," said Du Pré.

"Her mother's dead," said Harvey.

Du Pré looked at him.

"The only body we found," he said, "was hers. Now, if we just knew where Blackmore was, we could ask him about that."

Du Pré nodded.

"I will tell her," said Du Pré.

Harvey nodded.

"I don't think," he said, looking around at the mess, "that this is going to turn out well."

Du Pré looked off at the wreckage of the helicopter. It still smoldered.

"Three," said Harvey. "But they don't count."

"Travis?" said Du Pré.

Harvey nodded.

"We got Tomás's family," said Harvey. "Lew called somebody he knows down there in Torréon. Everybody's fine. The kid has talked to them by now. Good kid. Did us a great favor, and he gets enough green cards for it."

Du Pré laughed.

Harvey turned to him.

"Find that prick Blackmore," he said.

187

CHAPTER

39

Du Pré parked his cruiser on a side street and he went up the hill to the old brick hospital. Some of the patients were sitting outside smoking, and some were playing volleyball.

A nurse with a stethescope was taking vital signs at a picnic table. She would crook a finger at one or another of the volleyball players and that person would leave the game at once.

The nurse at the front desk listened to Du Pré and then she picked up the telephone and she spoke into it, and not long after a young woman in a long lab coat came out of the doors behind the front nurse's station.

"She said she would see you," said the young doctor. "I warn you, she isn't well. She might live, but I am not hopeful."

She led Du Pré down a long corridor of worn green tiles. She stood by the door.

Du Pré went in. Dora the cook was propped up in bed. She had an oxygen line under her nose and a couple of IVs in her arms. She smelled like very old booze sweated out.

Her eyes were huge and bright.

A buzzer sounded and the young doctor took off, her running shoes squeaking on the waxed linoleum.

"Du . . . Pré . . . ," Dora wheezed, "I can't breathe. These bastards won't give me a drink. It'd loosen me up."

Her belly was swollen with water.

She coughed, a wet choked sound.

Du Pré pulled up a chair. He took a small flask from the pocket of his jacket and he held the mouth to her lips. She drank slowly.

He put the flask back.

Dora coughed again. But there was a blush of pink in her cheeks now. She had been trembling and she had stopped.

"Whew," she said. "Miracle water, I allus called it."

Du Pré took the flask out, gave her some more.

"My liver's gone," said Dora. "But it put up a darned good fight."

Du Pré put the empty flask in his pocket.

"Blackmore," said Du Pré, "that plane, it was gone. Where else did he keep it?"

Dora looked at him.

"FBI," said Du Pré, "they raid three places, don't find it."

Dora laughed silently.

"Out near the breaks," said Dora, "there was an old potash mine. He had a hangar there, too. Used to take me there when he had his buddies come and they'd sit round drinking and admiring the plane. Had to fly it at night. He had a couple guys would set up those pots, the old ones that had the little flames like they used to put along the highway. He took me up there to cook. I remember once somebody asked if I was *reliable* . . . He said I was drunk all the time and plenty reliable. And they laughed. I was just another piece of kitchenware, like pots and pans."

"Where was it?" said Du Pré.

"I ain't sure," said Dora, "but he said it was near the place where

Granville Stuart hung everybody but Charley Rose, whoever that was."

Du Pré nodded.

"You know that place?" said Dora.

"Yah," said Du Pré. "The cattle thieves, they built a fort out of cottonwood logs. Stuart set it on fire, though. They ran out, he and his men shot most of them, wounded Charley, let him go because Charley's father was a banker, had some of Stuart's notes."

"Let the rich kid go and killed the poor boys," said Dora. "Ain't that about like it is."

"Yah," said Du Pré.

"Blackmore owned that place, but it was in someone else's name," said Dora. "He did that a lot, too."

Dora closed her eyes.

"I don't hurt," she said. "I will hurt soon's the booze wears off, but I don't now."

Du Pré took a silver flask out of his boot. It was flat and long and curved.

He slid it under the bedclothes. Dora's hand touched his.

"Du Pré," she said, "could you kiss me on the forehead? I think I am going soon. My daddy always kissed me on the forehead when he tucked me in bed."

Du Pré stood up, leaned over, kissed her pale sweaty skin.

Her breath was coming in quick short gasps now.

Du Pré took the flask back, slid it into his boot, left the room. He looked down the hall.

It was empty.

He went back in and unplugged the monitor line.

Dora was gasping.

He went back out and down the hall and out a side door then, and he got into the cruiser.

He looked at his watch.

He squinted at the sun.

He drove north for a while and then he turned east and let the old cruiser get up to speed.

The two-lane blacktop stretched toward the pale tan and violet horizon.

Near dark he stopped at a roadhouse and got two cheeseburgers and two fifths of bourbon to go.

The cell phone in the glove box chirred.

Du Pré ignored it for a while, but it would not stop.

He took it out and opened it and pressed the button.

"I just knew you were there," said Harvey.

"Yah," said Du Pré.

"We have about a thousand people looking for that fucking airplane," said Harvey, "but I thought I would call my good old buddy Du Pré and find out where it is."

"Don't know," said Du Pré.

"The jerks at Blackmore's main ranch don't know anything," said Harvey. "Even with sodium pentothal they don't know anything."

"Yah," said Du Pré. "They don't know anything. Me, I do not know, either."

"You ain't at home with Madelaine," said Harvey. "You know something."

"*Non,*" said Du Pré.

Du Pré heard someone talking to Harvey, but he couldn't make out the words.

"You goddamned half-breed son of a bitch," said Harvey. "You found that drunken cook, Dora McMasters."

"Yah," said Du Pré.

"She died," said Harvey. "Not long after you left."

"Oh," said Du Pré.

Du Pré saw a pullout by the road on the other side. There was a big semi there, the driver checking the tires. Du Pré turned in and he stopped and got out.

"I am going to put a trace on this phone," said Harvey. "They work even if the phone isn't turned on."

"Non," said Du Pré. "I am maybe hundred miles east of Great Falls, headed there."

"I am still doing the trace," said Harvey, "if you won't tell me where the plane is."

"I don't know," said Du Pré.

"Call me," said Harvey.

Du Pré shut the phone up. The driver was on the other side of the rig.

Du Pré jammed the phone into a roll of the hay the trailer carried.

He walked back to his cruiser and got in and headed east.

CHAPTER

40

The old road snaked north in pale winds, the starlight making it shimmer a little.

Du Pré got out of the old cruiser.

He knelt and he looked at the bare earth.

A beetle wandered past, sensed Du Pré, hiked its ass in the air.

Du Pré stood up. The breeze from the north smelled of dust and the river.

Wide Missouri.

He got back in the cruiser and he drove on, with no lights. It was easy to see the road.

He stopped and backed the car into the shadow of a chimney of rock.

He opened the trunk and took out moccasins and he pulled off his boots and put on the Cree shoes, ones that laced at the back.

He rubbed dirty oil from the engine on his face, put his hat in the car, tied a dark blue kerchief round his head. He put four magazines in his coat pockets, a flask, some chocolate. A small but very powerful flashlight.

The wind changed.

Du Pré smelled rain to the west.

He looked up at the stars. Faint high wisps of white shuddered across the studded black.

He trotted up the road, and when he got near the top of the hill he went on hands and knees to a stone piled with others, an Indian lookout, more than a century old.

The old mine was up against a bluff down in a long narrow valley below, out of the wind.

There was a giant metal building that had some of the steel sheets waving loosely in the breeze.

The metal crumpled, boomed, like distant thunder.

Du Pré saw a flare of light.

Someone had lit a cigarette. That person was in the shadows near the cavernous opening in the near end of the building. The huge doors that slid along overhead tracks were shoved back. One had jumped off the track and sat oddly angled against the tall wall.

There were lights in the building, greenish, not too strong.

Two men appeared in the doorway. The man in the shadows joined them.

Du Pré slipped down the hillside, going from shadow to sagebrush, sometimes wriggling snakelike on his belly.

He got to the bottom of the hill. It was a quarter mile or so to the big metal building.

There was ample cover, and Du Pré was close enough to see inside in half an hour.

A bright light flooded the huge building, and Du Pré could see the airplane, all black but for the clear Perspex windows.

Two men were fueling the airplane, from fifty-five-gallon drums on the back of a flatbed truck.

Son of a bitch, Du Pré thought, I got no explosive. Aviation fuel, though, it will do.

A man dressed in camouflage stepped out of the huge doorway, and he had a submachine gun on a sling round his neck and black goggles. When they turned toward Du Pré the lenses glowed green.

Du Pré froze. He had a sagebrush between himself and the door.

Night vision goggles.

Thunder rumbled close behind Du Pré. The storm had moved very close. There was a flash to the west, and after some seconds the boom of thunder.

Ten minutes, Du Pré thought.

He checked his pistol and the MP-40.

Wish I had tracers.

An alarm began to blat and screech, and the man in the shadows appeared suddenly, and he cut loose with a burst from his machine pistol.

Slugs whapped through the sagebrush around Du Pré.

The men fueling the plane pulled the hose back, and one stepped on a wing to close the port.

Du Pré saw two men in leather jackets and old-fashioned leather flying helmets step up on the wing and lift up the Perspex and they got in. Another man went in through a door in the rear.

The truck with the fuel drums drove out of the building, right at Du Pré, and the man driving it parked the truck and the lights went off.

The engines of the P-38 burst into life, roaring and thundering, unmuffled.

The plane's twin propellors began to turn, and it moved slowly to the open door.

"There!" someone shouted. "There!" and a burst of slugs spattered around Du Pré.

Bastard with the night vision goggles was behind the truck.

Du Pré rolled to a hollow and he lay facedown while bullets went *crack* overhead or chewed leaves and branches from the sagebrush. The torn bushes smelled sweet.

The engines of the plane roared louder, the revolutions rising and rising, the airplane screaming with furious power.

Du Pré rolled again, set the machine pistol to his shoulder, and another burst of fire made him drop down and try to claw into the earth again.

The plane was roaring down the dirt runway. It had no lights, but pale blue flames shot out of the exhausts.

Du Pré rolled, came half up, saw the two men, fired, the slugs caught them and shoved them back like fists punching. They fell, boneless.

There was a great crack overhead and the sky was bright for a moment, and then a furious wind stirred up dirt and grass.

There was a sound of an engine winding as it climbed, the sound of a truck on a hill.

Du Pré stuck his head up, looked.

The lights were still on in the building.

The two men he had shot lay there.

He stood up.

He smelled smoke, saw a flicker in the pile of drums on the back of the flatbed truck.

Du Pré dove for the ground as the fuel drums blew. The empty ones popped and the full ones stood for a moment until the pressure shoved fuel out, and then feathers of flame glowed.

Du Pré ran.

The drums behind him blew up, no pattern to it, and cast flaming fuel for hundreds of feet in all directions.

Du Pré ran and ran and he fell, his foot catching something.

The aviation fuel raged on, the rain hardly damping the fires.

Du Pré watched the building for a while. Then a couple of drums of fuel blew, and the concussion shoved at the old building, and it cracked and creaked and swung round on its foundations, and then it settled and the lights inside went out.

Du Pré walked back to his cruiser. He put the MP-40 in the rawhide case in the trunk and he had about half of a bottle of bourbon.

He was almost to the two-lane blacktop when a spotlight pinned his cruiser.

A man got out of the helicopter while it hovered, and he ran hunched over, wary of the blades, and when he got to Du Pré, he stood up.

"You miserable half-breed son of a bitch," said Harvey Wallace.

CHAPTER
41

"As it happens," said Foote, his voice on the telephone sounding very lawyerly, "she is a resident of Illinois and so this office will take care of it. She will be an emancipated minor. With both parents dead and grandfather a fugitive on federal warrants, it will not be difficult."

"OK," said Du Pré.

"If she wants to stay with Jacqueline and Raymond, she can, or she can go someplace else."

"She and Lourdes are girls who like horses," said Du Pré. "I think it is the horses that matter."

"Poor kid," said Foote. "I see that the number of lawsuits filed against the ATF has topped two hundred, and since there are far more suspects than crimes to charge them with, I expect it will be no end of embarassment. Most of the weapons were legal anyway. The Apache was not, but I doubt much will come of that. The Pentagon does not wish it known that though one may not buy an attack helicopter, one can buy all of the parts."

"Pret' stupid," said Du Pré.

"Speaking as one who had a short career in a government agency," said Foote, "the imbecility and squalid ass-covering is . . . superb."

"Superb," said Du Pré.

"Peerless," said Foote. "Now, I have yet to talk with Harvey, who I understand is much put out with the lovely Samantha Pidgeon, who is, bless her, very fond of Bart."

"Yah," said Du Pré.

"She shot down the helicopter with Travis in it, and Harvey did so want to talk to him," said Foote. "He's beside himself."

"He live," said Du Pré.

"So, my friend," said Foote, "now how will you go about finding Blackmore and that antique airplane?"

"Maybe I don't," said Du Pré. "Maybe I drink my whiskey, smoke, watch my grandkids have fun, play my fiddle."

"Of course," said Foote. "How could I have thought otherwise?"

They talked a few more minutes about nothing much and Du Pré hung up.

"We go now," said Madelaine. "We are late, you are late."

They went out and down the street to the Toussaint Saloon, Du Pré carrying the fiddle in the old rawhide case Catfoot had made over seventy years before.

The bar was full of people.

Bassman was outside finishing a spliff the size of a hammer handle.

The sweet smoke rose up toward the paling light.

He nodded as they walked past.

Père Godin was on the little stage, fingering the keyboard of his accordion.

"Old goat," said Madelaine. "How many children you have now this day?"

"Forty-one," said Père Godin. "Them two girls each have twins."

Du Pré laughed.

"How you keep track of them?" said Madelaine.

"Pins," said Père Godin. "I got this map, put pins in it."

Madelaine went to help Susan Klein with the drinks and Du Pré made himself a tall ditch and he drank it and made another and he went to the stage and he took out the fiddle and he tuned it. Only the A string was out a little.

Père Godin sent a riff of tumbling notes from his accordion out into the room and Du Pré put the fiddle to his chin and he answered, and they slid into a long instrumental, dabs of melody asked and answered.

Bassman came in and Du Pré launched "Baptiste's Lament" and they played it through and then they began a jig and people got up and went to the little dance floor and began to two-step around while still laughing and talking.

Jacqueline and Raymond and most of the kids came in, Lourdes and Anne-Marie together, dressed in riding boots and new hats.

Young women, soon the boys come, maybe they already have.

Bart and Pidgeon were in the corner, Pidgeon dressed as quietly as possible, but her beauty was the sort that gathers light, and men kept stealing glances at her. Bart looked like he couldn't believe his luck.

Me, I do not believe it, either.

They finished the first set and took a break and Bassman went out to bring his ganja level up to normal for his age and body weight.

Père Godin was charming a young woman Du Pré had never seen before.

Forty-two, few months, old goat.

Du Pré went to the bar and he got a drink and he went outside to cool off. The bar was so crowded with people it was steamy and close.

Madelaine appeared beside him, holding a big glass of pink fizzy wine and she rubbed Du Pré's neck with her free hand.

"You done good," she said.

Du Pré shrugged.

"They find him, they are looking," she said.

"Crazy man with machine guns," said Du Pré. "Ver' bad airplane he has, too."

"They find him," said Madelaine.

After a while they went back inside and Du Pré and Père Godin and Bassman played for an hour.

They took another break.

"Where is your woman?" said Du Pré.

"Home," said Bassman. "Keeping the kid in the school, it is a big job, that, has to march her there and back, five days a week."

Du Pré laughed.

"Good kid," said Bassman. "I think anyway."

"Good like you," said Du Pré.

"I have me for a kid, I shoot me," said Bassman. "I am little bastard when I am a kid, my parents both die young and happy they don't got, deal with me anymore."

Du Pré laughed.

"Good place this, good people," said Bassman. "That old man him here looking for you before you come."

"Benetsee?" said Du Pré.

"Him," said Bassman. "See him drift past. Him come back."

Maybe not. I go there, we are done.

They went back in and played the last set and Bassman took his money and headed for Turtle Mountain.

Père Godin went off with the young woman no one had seen before.

Du Pré helped Madelaine and Susan and Benny clean up.

He hauled a big bag of empty beer cans out back.

Benetsee was standing there.

He had no paint on now.

The old man grinned. His mouth held a few stubby blackened teeth.

He threw something at Du Pré's feet. A hairy thing, gray and smelling of smoke.

Du Pré picked it up.

A scalp.

CHAPTER
42

They left before dawn, Du Pré and Booger Tom mounted, Benetsee trotting on ahead, his old legs pumping tirelessly.

They went through the huge pasture that sat on the benchland and then they started up the trail into the Wolf Mountains, Benetsee leading the way.

The trail was wet. It had rained a lot up here the night before.

The horses slipped from time to time, the footing treacherous.

Benetsee trotted along, surefooted as a mountain goat.

The going was slow and after they got to the pocket valley halfway up the flank of Cooper Mountain the horses were sweating, so they stopped to cool them off.

Du Pré and Booger Tom pulled up bunches of grass dry from the sun to rub the horses down with.

Du Pré had a pull from his flask and he offered it to Booger Tom, who shook his head.

"End of the day," the old man said. "I would get tired if I did that now."

Benetsee had disappeared.

"You know where we are goin'?" said Booger Tom. "That spooky old bastard has turned hisself into a bird again, prolly."

Du Pré laughed.

A huge raven flew past lazily, gliding overhead and then down the trail they had come up.

"Lost Horse Meadow," said Du Pré.

Booger Tom nodded.

"I thought so," he said. "I suppose it could be worse, could be over the top and down the other side."

They went on for another couple of hours, and then stopped to eat and let the horses crop some grass and rest.

"I was a young man," said Booger Tom, "I dreamed about country like this, and now that I am old I still do."

The mountain fell away, the slopes dark with fir and pine, to the far plains below, stretching south in rolls and folds a hundred miles.

"Mist over the river," said Booger Tom. "Missouri's gonna have some rain tonight."

They went on and halfway to sundown they got to the long meadow, a narrow valley nearly at timberline, thick with grass.

A grizzly eating roots looked up, snorted, ran down the mountain to the timber. He crashed through the lodgepole, squirrels complained.

The wind changed. They smelled the burnt rubber and flesh and metal.

A wing lay propped up against a rock. Just beyond it the black char began, the deep scar in the soil where the plane had hit and then burned.

The wreckage was laid out for half a mile.

Du Pré smelled rotting human flesh.

There were two charred corpses still strapped in seats a few feet apart. The fire had burned hot, the bodies were black and shrunken.

The third body was in pieces, the man in the back of the plane.

Du Pré bent down over one of the bodies still strapped to a seat. Not much to recognize.

"What the hell was he doin' here?" said Booger Tom.

"Ask him," said Du Pré. "He has time, answer."

The mountain peaks rose up around them, an eagle soared on an updraft.

Du Pré took out a satellite telephone and he dialed.

The telephone rang and rang and then Harvey answered.

"We found him," said Du Pré.

"Where?" said Harvey. "Don't you dare kill him."

"Him dead," said Du Pré. "Him crash his plane behind us, the Wolf Mountains."

Harvey was silent.

"What was he doing there?" he said.

"Crashing the airplane," said Du Pré.

"You can wait there? Till I get some people there?" said Harvey.

"*Non,*" said Du Pré. "It is at the head of Long Meadow Valley, it is on the maps, Cooper Mountain, Long Meadow Valley. They are not going anywhere. Bad burned."

"The old man," said Harvey.

"Yah," said Du Pré. "Him bring me Blackmore's scalp."

"Jesus," said Harvey.

"Him, joke a lot," said Du Pré.

"Yeah," said Harvey, "he does."

"We go now," said Du Pré. "Not that much light."

They started back in the warm sun, and it had dried the trail enough so they made very good time. The horses were hungry and wanted to be in the barn with oats and hay.

They got to the ranch at sundown.

Two helicopters had gone over an hour before, headed up high.

Du Pré and Booger Tom put the horses up and they went to Bart's house.

Pidgeon answered the door.

She looked at them.

She stood aside and they came in.

Bart was in the kitchen, cooking Chinese food.

"Well?" said Pidgeon.

"Blackmore, two other guys, are dead. Plane went into the mountain."

Pidgeon grinned.

Bart looked at her.

"The woman," he said, "is merciless. She wants all bad guys dead."

Du Pré laughed.

"She, my Madelaine, should talk," he said.

"I believe," said Bart, "that they do."

They all laughed.

Du Pré and Booger Tom drank whiskey.

"He did it," said Pidgeon. "That old man did that. I don't know how, but he did it."

Du Pré nodded.

"Who is he?" said Pidgeon.

"Him old, my father Catfoot is young," said Du Pré.

Pidgeon poured herself some wine and Bart some mineral water.

"I'd like to know," she said.

"Maybe not," said Du Pré.

"Blackmore couldn't have gone much of anywhere," said Pidgeon, "He had the plane hidden someplace, but he was running. I wonder where?"

"Maybe there is something, the plane," said Du Pré.

"It is over, isn't it?" said Bart.

Pidgeon went to him, ruffled his hair.

"It isn't ever over, love," she said.

Bart looked sad.

"The girls are racing Saturday," said Bart.

"Yes, honey," said Pidgeon. "That they are."

The telephone rang. Madelaine answered, talked a moment, nodded to Du Pré.

He took the thing in his hand, put it to his ear.

"Yah," he said.

"It is your Auntie Pauline," said Auntie Pauline.

"I am sorry," said Du Pré. "We don't know who killed Badger."

"He is dead," said Auntie Pauline. "Poor Badger, I cannot help him, but I am going to Paris."

"Oh," said Du Pré.

"I meet this nice man," said Auntie Pauline.

EPILOGUE

Ten Months Later

Du Pré saw the four vehicles parked at the end of the dirt track.

Harvey was standing by a government SUV. He had on jeans and hiking boots and a wind breaker.

It was a brisk chilly day, sunny and beautiful.

A prairie falcon shot past.

Du Pré got out, nodded.

"You been here before?" said Harvey.

Du Pré nodded.

"Buffalo Calf Butte," he said. "Sacred place. I come here once with Catfoot, my grandfather, I am maybe four years old."

"But you remember it?" said Harvey.

Du Pré nodded.

They walked up the winding trail that led to the flat top of the stone fortress. It rose up a hundred feet from the plains, walls sheer save for one place water had cut a gentler angle. The trail went up that, over the slabs of spalled rock that frost had pried away from the cliff.

Harvey was wheezing.

Du Pré sat down, rolled a cigarette.

"Asshole," said Harvey.

Du Pré nodded.

"He was easy enough to identify," said Harvey. "Had his wallet in his flight suit and his watch on his wrist. Ferris Blackmore. The scalp you said Benetsee gave you? DNA said that was Blackmore's, too. We checked that out months ago."

"Maybe Benetsee," said Du Pré. "Maybe a coyote."

"The corpses up on the mountain in the wreckage of that P-38 were the two Irish thugs and Blackmore's pilot. Blackmore bailed out of the plane. Or was there another plane he bailed out of?"

Du Pré shrugged.

"That spooky old bastard could have told us where he got the damned scalp," grumbled Harvey. "He really could have."

"Benetsee," said Du Pré, "him, he likes his jokes."

"Till we got the lab tests back I was not wanting to think the old bastard flew up to the P-38, got in, scalped Blackmore, and flew back down with his scalp. You may well imagine my relief when we found Blackmore was not there."

Du Pré nodded.

"His parachute was all gathered," said Harvey, "by the book, and weighted down with rocks. Birds and coyotes ate his meat and tossed his bones around."

"That," said Du Pré, "is what they do. They are there for that."

"So," said Harvey, "all I have to believe now is that Benetsee was waiting for Blackmore up there, knew he'd land there, which is not a whole lot of comfort."

"Benetsee," said Du Pré, "him not a comfortable person."

They went on, scrambled up the last fifteen feet, came out on the flat top. There were seven other people there. Sheriff's deputy, some FBI suits, a coroner, a couple ambulance orderlies.

"We could be looking at something," said Harvey, "and not see it."

Du Pré nodded.

He started at the shredded flight suit, ripped and torn by the coyotes, and he spiraled out and away from that. The skull grinned from a cleft between two rocks. Femur, fibula, ribs, a foot-long section of Blackmore's spine.

Coyotes had dug at the earth here and there.

Du Pré saw the stone, a small flat greenish rock, not the rock of the butte.

It had been brought here.

He kept moving as he had, eyes down, came to the stone that sat on a flat slab. There were fire streaks on the slab, black carbon the winter and spring had not washed completely away.

Du Pré picked up the rock, found the black feather with the white tip under it. He palmed the feather, tossed the rock casually away. It clattered out of sight in a ruck of broken stones. He slipped the feather in his jacket pocket.

Du Pré kept walking slowly round and round.

The sun was getting hot.

Old man, old man, Du Pré thought, *you are some old bastard, yes . . .*